THE STEPMOTHER

BY THE SAME AUTHOR

The Harlequin Edition

THE
STEPMOTHER

Julian Fane

The Book Guild Ltd
Sussex, England

First published in Great Britain in 2003 by
The Book Guild Ltd
25 High Street
Lewes, East Sussex
BN7 2LU

Typesetting in Garamond by
Keyboard Services, Luton, Bedfordshire

Printed in Great Britain by
Antony Rowe Ltd, Chippenham, Wiltshire

A catalogue record for this book is available from
The British Library

ISBN 1 85776 723 3

This book is dedicated to the late JOHN GRIGG, unfailing friend

1

The Old Hundred at Luffield near Warminster
was a small manor house, and could well have
claimed that it was the most picturesque example of its much admired type.

Its front wall was dressed Bath stone and its
other walls were rough-hewn stones from the
Cotswolds, and its roof was made of stone
Cotswold tiles. The colour of the house was
golden, whatever the weather, and in early summer blue wisteria and in autumn red Virginia
creeper softened its outlines. It had large sash
windows, six bedrooms, and extra accommodation behind the dormer windows on its second
floor. It stood back from a quiet country road,
and its short straight drive was flanked by
paddocks with iron railings, usually occupied by
ponies with a donkey and a few sheep.

The village of Luffield was located in a dip in
the ground, not quite a valley, but its soil had
been enriched over the centuries by rainwater
and nutrients trickling down from higher ground
in the middle distance. Every growing thing did
well there, noticeably the trees on the ten acres
of Old Hundred land. The branches of a tremen-
dous sycamore provided shelter for animals in

the paddock on the right of the drive, and a stripling oak was large enough to hide the lean-to shed offering protection for livestock in the other one. There was a noble cedar of Lebanon on the lawn behind the house, and a fine array of forest trees complete with rookery in the grove beyond the gardens. An Irish yew flourished in the centre of the former farmyard, where the barn and sheds had been turned into garaging for cars and storage of horticultural machinery – the barn was now where chickens roosted and swifts and swallows built their nests.

The present occupants of this idyllic dwelling were the Crighton family, James and Veronica and their daughter and only child, Olive. Their ages were, respectively, sixty-nine, fifty-five and twenty-two.

James Crighton was not the owner of the house – it belonged to his wife. He had been born in humbler circumstances than those prevailing at The Old Hundred. He was the son of a pharmacist, who had risen so far in the world as to have his own chemist's shop in a back street of Bristol. James surpassed his parent by far with his scholarships, his qualification in Chartered Accountancy, his busy professional life, earning power, interest in politics, local to start with, then national, his thirty years in Parliament and his knighthood.

He had been a handsome younger man, blond, broad-shouldered, the Labrador type in canine terms, and always seemed to bear the brand of success. He was sharp if not exactly clever, let alone intelligent, and confident and altogether impressive. He could be charming, and he was tough. He was naturally drawn towards the Conservative Party, and he was quickly adopted by one of the Bristol constituencies. He won his seat in the first General Election he fought, and held on to it for nearly thirty years until he retired at sixty-five.

He had been in no hurry to marry. He reserved himself for the Miss Right who would deserve him until he was in his forties. His choice fell on Veronica Miller-Whitfield, a pretty dreamy unworldly twenty-six-year-old, whose double-barrelled name was gilt-edged and whose expectations in respect of The Old Hundred were seductive. The courtship was no whirlwind, more like a war of attrition. She was not attracted by his forcefulness, tactlessness, and public position and all it would entail. She was aware of yawning gaps between them – cultural, class. She felt that being fourteen years younger than he was, she did belong and would ever more clearly belong, to a different generation. But he wore down her resistance over many months, and when her parents died she agreed to let him take care of her, as he had repeatedly suggested.

Sir James Crighton boasted that he kept his word, and in one sense Lady Crighton benefited from his doing so. He was protective, faithful, financially independent, and maintained her property. He was a sort of rock, which was nice; but rocks are not particularly amusing to live with. Perhaps his best points in her eyes were that he seldom claimed his marital rights and otherwise let her lead her own life – he did not expect her to keep him company in his flat within range of the Division Bell or ask her too often to appear on his political platforms.

His retirement was a strain for both Crightons. He had suffered a mild heart attack and he followed the advice of his doctor reluctantly. For Veronica, the blow of having her active restless husband always at home fell sooner than she had bargained for. Olive, of course, was even more of a buffer and soothing influence than she had previously needed to be. And Denis Wilks, the Crightons' gardener, chauffeur, general handyman and old family friend, who lived in so-called Shepherd's Cottage attached to the farther end of the farmyard buildings, helped to alleviate the situation. Denis's wife Bertha had died shortly before his employer was meant to opt for the novelty of leisure, both men were startled to find themselves at loose ends, they put their heads together by tacit agreement and set to work on projects aimed at improving the amenities of The Old Hundred.

The daily round in the Crightons' home began at seven in the morning. At that hour Sir James was accustomed to rise and, even when he had nothing much he was obliged to do, could not break the habit. Besides, he liked to think he would have breakfast with his daughter.

Olive at seven left the narrow bed in the bedroom she had occupied since childhood, washed, dressed, put her two dogs out – her Cairn terrier Buddy and Whisper, a Ridgeback – and drank a quick cup of tea and ate some cereal in the kitchen before driving to the veterinary practice in Torton where she had worked as assistant to the vet since she left school.

Olive and her father kissed each other good morning, but their conversation was minimal.

'All well, darling?'

'Fine, Daddy. Are you all right?'

'Alive.'

'Funny Daddy.'

'Have something more to eat, my pet – you don't eat enough.'

'You've been saying that ever since I can remember. I must fly – see you this evening!'

James proceeded to make his breakfast of toast, fat-free spread, marmalade and decaffeinated coffee, then fetched the newspapers, read the bad news in his study and as usual wished he had not, attended to a few bills and at nine o'clock went out to join Denis and resume work on a drain they were repairing, or a wall that wanted repointing, or a replacement of the door to a shed, or a new pergola for roses.

Veronica left her bedroom, where she had slept alone for at least twenty years, round about nine, by which time Peggy Williams had arrived and was brewing proper coffee. Peggy lived in the village with her husband Joe, who had been a farm worker and was also now retired – he was a churchwarden and rang the church bell as required. She was a sweet kind red-faced woman and had been the Crightons' maid of all work since the year dot.

Again, as in the case of Denis, Peggy was more friend than employee. She and her 'M'lady' concocted a shopping list as they shared the coffee, then made the beds together, chatting. Later Veronica drove into Warminster, bought the necessary items, and was inevitably drawn towards bookshops and stores selling classical music recordings – books and opera could be called her passion, although she was not a temperamental person.

Peggy cooked lunch for the Crightons, and James would join Veronica rubbing his hands and repeating for the umpteenth time that he was turning into a 'horny-handed son of toil'. He had been hedging or ditching with Denis, and, having belatedly greeted his wife with an absent-minded peck on any facial area that was nowhere near her mouth, he tucked into his food and expatiated on the principles of using some rustic implement. If or when she could get a word in edgeways she would murmur, 'That's interesting ... I'm glad you're getting on so well with the work.'

It was an old story – she had been equally bored by his politics. But she was both thoughtful and lazy: she had better things to think about than his doings, and it saved her the trouble of talking when he held forth. Occasionally it crossed her mind that other wives would be more pleased with a husband who had earned a knighthood, was still good-looking with his fresh complexion and ample white hair, had recovered from life-threatening illness, and was never intentionally unkind. Although she was not discontented, and did not ask much more than to be allowed her privacy, at odd moments or at night she would wonder why she had missed out on the grand emotions she read about and liked to hear opera singers describe beautifully.

Her own strongest emotion was her maternal feeling for Olive and their loving friendship: the other side of the medal of which was that she hoped Olive was not too like herself, she feared that Olive's meekness and mildness might not bring her happiness, matrimonial or in another way, and that she had exerted a not altogether constructive influence over her daughter – James had often annoyed her by advising that the girl ought to get out more and meet boys, and to be quite the opposite of what she was.

After tea, while she waited for Olive to come home, she offered James at least her cooperation with his plans and preoccupations. In summer she would follow him out of doors to admire his scything of a patch of wild flowers or his building of a superfluous wall, and as the sun set and dusk fell they would return to the house, study their diaries and pencil in the social engagements which he had either arranged or was proposing. He counted on giving a dinner party for five or seven guests – eight or ten people including the three Crightons – once a fort-night, and occasionally inviting two or three people to lunch, neighbours, professional men. There were notes to be written and telephone calls to make; and because they entertained they were entertained, consequently letters of thanks for hospitality received were another of Veronica's duties.

These secretarial sessions stretched out in win-ter and strained Veronica's nervous system – she was easily tired by, as well as tired of, sociabili-ties, she dreaded any surfeit of strangers, whereas James was invigorated by social life, was always on the look-out for 'new' people, and was happy to discuss the seating of their guests until she was grinding her teeth with lack of enthusiasm.

Yet Veronica was not a rebellious wife. She gave James most of what he asked for. She would dress prettily for his parties and preside with poise and patience at her dining-room table at the head of which he sat. She did not mind him arrogating to himself the twin roles of master and owner of The Old Hundred – she had begun by correcting his references to 'my house', now she scarcely noticed them. That he was a good host of a bossy kind saved her trouble – she had no facile small talk, and invariably lost her voice by shouting and was deafened by the noisiness of people over-excited by food and wine.

'Hosting', the art of the host, James was pleased to think was one of his accomplish-ments. He would select topics to debate with his guests, and prepared solo performances to fill conversational gaps, statements of his political opinions, or the truth about scandals in the high places of yesteryear. One of his party pieces was to expatiate on the name of the house he lived in.

'Hundred is not only the number we were taught at school, it has a history reaching into the mists of time relative to property,' he would speechify. 'In the darkest ages it already referred to power, particularly the power conferred by the ownership of land. A primitive measurement of land was a hide, the hide of animal husbandry, and whoever could accumulate a hundred hides was automatically a leader of his community, expected to settle disagreements and dispense rough justice. Once upon a time our humble home here in Luffield was a courthouse, and Veronica's forebears differed from my gentle wife in that they served as local judge and jury and could have miscreants flogged and locked up. Later on, the farm attached to The Old Hundred was many hundreds of hides in size, but it was sold in one of the innumerable agricultural depressions, and the judicial function of the house was cancelled in the eighteenth century. There is a heavy tome waiting to be written about the changes that have occurred on our few acres, and I keep on telling my dearest daughter, its heiress presumptive, that she will one day be the trustee and guardian of a treasure-trove of the history of England.'

*   *   *

Veronica and Olive exchanged long-suffering glances when James gave tongue in this pompous manner.

Olive had never gone through the phase of girlish detestation of her parents. She had a few male friends, at work and in the village, but at first potential boyfriends found her too dignified and passive, then one or two men failed to notice that she worshipped them from afar. She always loved her mother and was resigned to being embarrassed by her father, and she wished to be nowhere but at The Old Hundred. She was an only child with a difference: as a result of wars, epidemics, accidents and follies, she had no grandparents, uncles, aunts or cousins by the time she was twenty years old.

Physically she was a slim girl with brown hair and blue eyes. More truthfully, she was skinny, her hair was straight and worn at an unbecoming length. Her working clothes were gumboots, corduroy trousers, and seasonal sloppy-joe knitwear or open-necked shirts, and in the evening at home she wore garments describable as either housecoats or dressing-gowns. Her smart attire for dinner parties or rare outings were a red velvet ankle-length dress or sleeveless summer numbers – neither looked good on her because they emphasised her angularity.

The most perspicacious criticism that could be levelled against her appearance was that she did not make the best of herself, for she lacked vanity to an almost dangerous degree, and almost hid her good points. For instance, she was well made, she had excellent proportions, and her gawkiness was also graceful. If or when she filled out she would have a pretty little figure, and if she cut her hair shorter she would show her neck to advantage. Subtly made up her complexion would improve, and less drab clothes would be a blessing.

The redeeming feature of Olive as she was, the feature defined to an unknown extent by her soul, was her smile. It was hard to understand, considering that her lips were not obviously kissable and her teeth were not perfectly straight; but her smile verged on a sort of beauty, it was like the light being switched on in a dark room, it dazzled harmlessly, and emitted messages of comprehension, comfort and cheer. Strange, too, that sudden illuminating smile of hers, since it bore resemblances to the smiling lips of her father and her mother without being either humourless or vague.

Olive's academic career was a sharp contradiction of the charge that she was subnormal. At her girls' boarding school she proved to be a bright pupil and was expected to go on to university. Instead, she not only wanted to work for a vet, she forced her father to cave in and allow her to do so. James could not overlook the fact that his daughter had a marked gift for making friends with animals, and Veronica, despite her cultural interests, was distrustful of bluestockings and always in favour of letting her daughter do as she pleased.

Buddy and Whisper, Olive's private pets,

superseded the rabbit, kitten, lamb and rescued mongrel she had loved and been loved by in earlier years. She did not take them to her place of work, where they might have contracted any number of infections; before leaving home in her Ford Fiesta she gave them a brisk walk, rain or shine. They then lounged about at The Old Hundred until she returned to feed them at lunchtime, and again awaited their second walk of the day in summer or winter evenings. Buddy was a biscuit-coloured Cairn, a small dog with a big personality, affectionate, courageous and bossy, whereas Whisper was a sleek beauty, as strong as she was gentle. The dogs slept in Olive's bedroom – not on her bed, in their baskets – and their good health and shining eyes attested for once to the unqualified success of an eternal triangle.

The vet who employed Olive, Tim Spell, dealt with canine and some of the agricultural business, and she looked after his paperwork, helped him with dogs' operations and general routine, and greeted their owners. Another vet, Jake Ould, and his assistant and visiting students, attended exclusively to farm-work and horses. The hours were often long and the labour hard, but Olive was tireless and stronger than she appeared to be – she was always carrying dopey Labradors or German Shepherds from the operating theatre to the recovery room. She was rewarded for her efforts by the dependence on her of her patients, the grateful licks of her hands, and the inspiration of the fine characters of most dogs in comparison with those of human and inhuman beings.

Joy may be an inflated word to associate with Olive's existence. She nonetheless rejoiced in her quiet way. For when she motored back to The Old Hundred at six o'clock or thereabouts, and after she had walked Buddy and Whisper for half an hour, she had her evening with her mother, with their music, and with the book she was reading, to look forward to.

The Crightons' home was by no means a low-toned dull place, whatever the impression it made on outsiders. Songs of love, arias bewailing in exquisite music the most terrible and tragic dramas of the heart, filled the drawing-room night after night and reduced Veronica and Olive to cathartic tears. James escaped to his study and then to bed – he was in no sense operatic, was tone-deaf, bored by love stories, and read only biographies of politicians. Veronica bought tapes and CDs, and when she and Olive had listened to them sufficiently they still had the pleasure of discussing them. Monteverdi and Mozart, Verdi, Puccini, Richard Strauss and Benjamin Britten, these were the subjects of their analysis and consideration, as other women dissect their friends and neighbours.

And at eleven or so, when Olive's dogs reminded them that the day was done, the two fond women would mount the stairs, talking, laughing in undertones so as not to disturb James, and kiss good night, happy in the knowledge that they were about to resume

13

their journey through the pleasure grounds of English literature that would lead to the Land of Nod.

People used to speak of the 'even tenor' of life, meaning the better days that have no history, the blessed intervals between storms and sorrows. Apart from James' heart attack and subsequent retirement, and from Olive's stubborn decision to devote herself to a job that struck some people, for example her father, as unworthy and demeaning, the tenor of nearly a quarter of a century of life at The Old Hundred merited the epithet 'even'. Since Olive was born, and further procreative activities ceased, the years had sped by in a discreet glow of contentment tinged with the glory of the vicarious excitements of opera and books. The Crightons had no money worries, lived in a house with an enviable exterior and a spacious interior, formed an almost self-sufficient group but had a wide enough circle of acquaintances, and were as well as could be expected considering age and minor medical setbacks. No wonder they were not exactly on their toes, ready to dodge the blows that fate usually delivers from unexpected angles, fate's 'sucker punches' that catch people off guard; nor were they prepared to be knocked flat by bad news or to somehow make the best of the worst. James was too sure that he could not be beaten, Veronica preferred not to bother her head with presentiments that might be a waste of emotion, and Olive understood the ills of dogs exclusively.

Anyway, if they privately went in for foresight they all happened to be looking in the wrong direction. James' heart did not stop beating, and Olive did not marry an unsuitable boy who aspired to be a vet one day. It was Veronica, who never exerted herself unduly, whose constitution bore comparisons with clockwork, who now, after a quite merry Christmas, lost weight and began to be sick.

Panic ensued. The health of James deteriorated in accordance with the tests Veronica was subjected to: his switch from unwise optimism to unyielding pessimism exerted a baleful influence on the whole household. Olive probably frightened her mother by giving up her work for the time being. Peggy the cook cried like a fountain, and Denis the gardener never stopped declaiming rhetorically 'Oh dear!' in thunderous accents as he worked in and out of the house.

Terminal cancer was diagnosed. Veronica was only half-told the truth by her doctors, but her husband's tears, her daughter's ashen face and everybody's consternation rendered all her possible questions superfluous.

She responded to her situation characteristically, without rebelliousness. She did not feel too bad until nearly the end of her illness, but grew thinner and weaker day by day. At length the attempts to arrest the cancer were abandoned, and she spent her days in bed at The Old Hundred.

As often as possible, mother and daughter conspired together to banish James from her bedroom so that they could listen to some of their music. Olive censored the famous death scenes, but Veronica smiled her acknowledgement of the considerate thought while also shrugging her shoulders feebly as if to indicate that she was past caring one way or the other.

Olive maintained her vigil day and night for getting on for six weeks. She waited on her mother, nursed her as best she could, talked as required in quiet tones, and held the pale and wasted hand. Veronica's courage was exemplary and influential, but caused all the people around her to be even more sorry they were losing her.

One day she said to Olive: 'Life goes too quickly, I never had time to appreciate my life.'

On another day she said: 'I won't make such a good death as Violetta or Mimi.'

'No, no, Mother – better,' Olive tried to reply.

At the start of the last week Veronica grew agitated in the night and eventually whispered to Olive: 'I'm feeling guilty, I haven't done any of the things people ought to do, and now I can't, I'm so sorry that I can't.'

'What do you mean, Mother?'

'I haven't made a new will.'

'Don't worry, please – nothing like that matters.'

'Your father knows that our home belongs to you.'

'I'm sure he does – don't worry.'

16

'I'll tell him again.'

'Not for my sake – Daddy and I, we'll fix everything.'

'Will you? Don't forget, darling – it's yours.'

'No, I won't.'

'Give money to Peggy and Denis, won't you?'

'Of course.'

'Thank you – and forgive me.'

'Nothing, nothing to forgive.'

A day or two later Veronica was also worried that she was wearing Olive out, and asked for a professional nurse. The Crightons' doctor, Dr Wood, sent along a young woman called Angela who took charge and rearranged things more comfortably for her patient.

The funeral was a miserable affair. James could not deal with the practicalities and Olive had none of the requisite experience. The service was left to the vicar and the undertaker, and there was no wake at The Old Hundred.

Angela Malone cried a lot and distributed warm hugs and kisses as she drove away, and James and Olive were alone.

2

If the death of Veronica Crighton was one surprise, to put it objectively and callously, what
became of James after she died was another.

He went to pieces. His heart was broken,
Peggy Williams reiterated, a description surpris-
ing inasmuch as he had seemed to have a heart
only in the cardiac context. His health did not
suffer noticeably, he retained his clear eye and
pink cheeks, yet grew increasingly apathetic. A
practical man, he could no longer cope with
simple physical tasks and was sometimes suspected of shamming, for he could shave himself
but was incapable of making a telephone call.
He sat in his study staring into space, while the
correspondence piled up on his desk and tradespeople called at the house for the settlement of
bills he had omitted to pay.

He was not silenced by his state of mind. He
spoke to Olive, and insisted on her listening to
his mournful refrain. His analyses of his condi-
tion were rational, if exaggerated. Veronica had
complemented him, he explained, had truly
been his better half, and he was nothing that
was worth anything without her. He was a fail-
ure, his relentless activities had been sound and

fury that signified damn all, whereas her private life was flower-like, its nature had been to bring beauty into the view of her family and the world in general. She was irreplaceable, he said over and over again, and he could not see his way ahead, unlit by her company and the glow of her soul.

Veronica's irreplaceability was a figment of his imagination. Olive's soul might not have glowed, but she was forced to take over her mother's duties, to pay much more attention to her father than her mother ever had, and to cope with the affairs of the head of the house and the posthumous legal procedures. She had to ask for more time away from her work with Tim Spell. She walked Buddy and Whisper hurriedly so as not to be absent from The Old Hundred for too long. Her own grief was postponed.

When she registered her mother's death in Warminster, she also bravely called in at the offices of Tyndall and East, the Crightons' solicitors for donkeys' years. She saw Mr Martin East, son of Robin who had founded the business, and in reply to some of his queries asked if he could possibly come to The Old Hundred and attempt to get proper answers from her father.

Mr East duly turned up by appointment. Olive ushered him into the study, but was not allowed to escape. Her father called her back, said he was seeing no solicitor on his own, and embarrassed her to the point of mortification during the triangular conference that ensued.

Mr East was youngish, polite and sympathetic. He began by offering Sir James condolences.

'I'm finished, you know,' James replied. 'No use you talking to me. What do you want?'

'My wish is not to upset you, sir, but there are some legal matters to be cleared up, as I'm sure you will understand.'

'My daughter can see to all that.'

'Miss Crighton felt that you should be consulted, sir.'

'She's wrong. You're wrong, my dear. I can't speak for her. She owns everything. That's all I have to say.'

'Please, Daddy!'

'Oh well – fire away – more hot air!'

'Sir, we have a will made by Lady Crighton before her marriage to yourself, bequeathing to you the residue of her estate.'

'Oh God!'

'I beg your pardon, sir, but do you have knowledge of any other will?'

Olive spoke up: 'She told me there was no new will.'

'Look here!' James exclaimed. 'Look, I'm handing everything over to my daughter as soon as I can get round to it. My wife meant me to, she told me on her death-bed.'

'In that case, sir, estate duty would be levied on the fortune, whereas no estate duty is payable between husband and wife.'

'It's six of one and half a dozen of the other. Don't complicate the issue! How many years, how many weeks, do you imagine I'll be sitting here? When I die taxes will have to be paid, that's one certainty – why hang around? I'll do the right thing while I'm able, and give The Old Hundred to the person it belongs to.'

'Daddy, please!'

'Don't object, my darling, don't be silly – I'm talking sense for a change. I won't live long enough to qualify for one of those fancy schemes that cheat the taxman.'

'Be that as it may, Sir James, I would advise you to consider such a scheme in view of the considerable value of the estate. There will have to be a valuation for probate to legalise the transfer of the property, and a valuation would give a clear picture of the sums of money involved.'

'Go ahead! But your work must aim for getting everything into Olive's name with the minimum delay. Bring me figures, if you like, but I can't guarantee to look at them. I don't want to own anything that isn't mine for a day more than's unavoidable. Thank you. Goodbye!'

Olive escorted Mr East to the front door.

'Miss Crighton, shall I arrange for valuers to come here, or will you?'

'Please don't call me Miss Crighton, please call me Olive.'

'And I'm Martin East. I hope you'll call me Martin.'

'I'm sorry about my father. He's not himself, honestly he isn't. I'd much rather you looked after everything.'

'As you say. But I wonder if your father might

be prepared to give you or my firm a power of attorney, that is authority to deal with all business matters, subject to your agreement.'

'I don't know. I can't ask him questions any more. I'll have to leave it to you. My job is to look after dogs.'

The sum of money thrown up by the valuation of The Old Hundred, Shepherd's Cottage, the buildings around the farmyard and various sheds, the garden, paddocks, and contents of the house, furniture, pictures, silver, Lady Crighton's jewellery and her securities, was so large that the notion of having nearly half of it confiscated by the government roused James to the point of resolving to do nothing in a hurry.

The negative course of action suited his listless mood. Martin East respected Olive's wish that no issue should be forced for the time being. James confined his references to the subject to calling himself his daughter's tenant.

Four weeks after the funeral Olive was still at home. Tim Spell had found a veterinary student who was helping in her absence, but she was afraid she might never get back to work or else that Tim would have to employ her replacement permanently. Whenever she hoped to return in a day or two, another crisis developed, and then she had to ring Tim, explain, apologise and renew promises she was not sure she could keep.

The shock waves of her mother's death spread through the house like an infection. Peggy suf-

fered with her nerves and was apt to ring at the
crack of dawn to say she was staying at home
for the day: 'Cooking would make me sick, Miss
– I feel so shook up.' Denis said he had lost the
will to work, and announced that he was unable
to feed the animals in the paddock – 'I haven't
the strength, the garden's more than I should be
doing now Sir James has packed in'. He said the
sheep should go to market, and his earthy advice
was to have the ponies and donkey taken to the
knacker's yard.

Olive consequently shopped, cooked and
attended to her four-legged retainers, and tried
to get a grip on the wages of those with two
legs, and puzzle out their overtime and tax, and
then persuade her father to sign the requisite
cheques.

James was no better. Emotionally he was
worse, although he now read newspapers, and
tottered into the garden to talk to Denis. His
grieving had lurched in a conscience-stricken
direction. He blamed himself for having been
unworthy of his wife. He had been incapable of
accompanying her into the realms of art, and a
millstone round her neck. When Olive contra-
dicted him, he cried irritably, metaphorically he
stamped his foot; and she could not help reflect-
ing that he was running true to form in that his
self-centredness had resurfaced.

Another alteration had occurred in his attitude to the monetary side of Veronica's estate.
He was loath to spend the money in the account
that held the wherewithal to pay household

expenses. He swore to Olive that it was not because he was mean, on the contrary it was for her sake, because the major part of the money rightly belonged to her and he was doing his best not to squander her inheritance. As a result, he made her requests for essential funds into an ordeal, and left her feeling like a beggar. Needless to say, she did not like to ask him for a lump sum – her parents had never given her any money to speak of, her mother had never thought of doing so – and now her father, despite his scruples in respect of her rights, was pauperising her.

She received telephone calls from Martin East from time to time, requesting her assistance over documents that had to be signed by her father. One day he rang up, inquired about her health and welfare, and as she had just emerged from a bruising session in the study her answer was to cry.

Martin drove over to see her that afternoon. He guessed so much that she told him the rest of the story. He was shocked to hear that she was penniless, in fact overdrawn at the bank, for her wages had been her income, Tim Spell could not afford to pay her for not working, and she had used up her savings. He then managed to persuade her to let him have a shot at making sense of the situation.

Olive warned her father that Martin East had urgent business to discuss with him, and shut the two men together in the study with a shaky hand.

She overheard the first exchanges.

'You made no appointment.'

'I believe you will agree that I had no time to notify you, Sir James. I have reason to believe you are in danger of losing your gardener and your cook-housekeeper.'

'What are you talking about?'

'Their wages can no longer be paid, sir.'

'Olive sees to that.'

'Olive has run out of money, sir.'

'But I give her money as she needs it.'

'I beg your pardon, Sir James, I have been speaking to Olive...'

She could not bear to listen any longer. The last thing she had ever wanted to be was a bone of contention. She walked about in an anguished manner, alternately stopping her ears and wringing her hands.

Martin found her and waved a sheet of paper in her direction. She succeeded in reading that her father was transferring twenty thousand pounds into her account. She cried again, and Martin helped to comfort her with his arm round her shoulders. She thanked him very much indeed and they said goodbye.

A quarter of an hour later she had summoned up enough courage to face her father. He was waiting for her, still sitting at his desk where he had signed his name. Dusk was falling out of doors, only the desk light was switched on, and he looked ancient. To make matters worse he sobbed at the sight of her, lowered his head and began to mumble between hiccups.

'Why didn't you tell me? You don't trust me. I'm ruining your life. I'd die if I could, and you'd be rid of me.'

She thanked him, denied his charges and begged him not to be sad. She could not bring herself to hold him in her arms or dry his eyes, and cursed herself for being shy of physical contact with him, and wished she had gone bankrupt for his sake and therefore would not have to put up with this woeful and hateful rigmarole.

'You'll feel better soon, Daddy,' she said hopefully.

But she was wrong. He continued to catalogue his failures masochistically and with mounting excitement.

'I've done even worse for you than I did for your mother. It never occurred to me that you were short of money. I've disgraced myself. Oh God, let me die! Don't thank me – the twenty thousand's yours, and it'll be free of tax, no tax payable, they say. Oh my darling! How could such a bad father have such a good daughter? I'll leave you in peace soon, as soon as ever I can. Behave as if I'm dead, please! Get away from here, from me, and live your own life!'

He was unstoppable. Olive feared he would have another heart attack or a stroke. She could not promise, as repeatedly implored, to resume her work and desert him for five days a week.

At last she had a brainwave and said she would see if Angela happened to be available.

* * *

Angela was, and arrived at The Old Hundred the next afternoon. Olive was waiting for her, they embraced on the gravel sweep as Angela stepped out of her battered Honda Civic, and, when Buddy and Whisper and their acquaintance of not so long ago had exchanged greetings, the two women strolled to and fro in the drive, swapping information. Angela seemed to understand Olive before the latter had finished speaking.

'Poor dear man,' she commented. 'The poor old ones are always better with people who are not members of the family. I've a soft spot for Sir James, I have, and I'll cheer him up by hook or crook. You can leave him to me while you go about your business, I'll take care of him, never fear.'

Luck figured in their conversation.

Olive said: 'I know how lucky we are to have caught you just when you were between jobs,' and Angela echoed her thus: 'It's my luck to be back in your lovely home and with such a charming family. I've thought of you often since I was here with your mother. Your family's my ideal of how real ladies and gentlemen live – no, honestly, I'm not flattering. In my line of work I have to look after all sorts, but seldom anyone so gracious as you were to me the first time round. Thank you for remembering me.'

Angela had been living in digs in Bath while she worked in the Bath hospitals or nursing homes. When Olive contacted her, she was taking a few days off, so had to cancel nothing in order to come to Luffield, and there were no commitments hanging over her future.

Olive ventured to mention payment for Angela's services. A frightening sum was mentioned and immediately modified in the following generous way.

'I don't belong to any agency, I used to but now I prefer to hang on to my money, not pay a big percentage of it to the middlemen – pigs in the middle, I call them. Besides, I don't need agents – nurses can always earn their keep. Agency fees are exorbitant in my opinion. Here I don't suppose I'll be doing any serious nursing yet – why not think of me as your carer, because I do care for your family? That means we could cut agency fees almost in half. Could you afford such a weekly sum without straining?'

Olive thanked her and replied: 'I haven't thought of the time scale. My father talks about dying. If he doesn't die we might have to review expenditure and everything.'

'Of course. Shall we play it by ear? But remember, I don't need notice if or when the job comes to an end – you can tip me the wink and I'll fly away.'

Olive referred to her difficulties with Buddy and Whisper.

Angela said: 'I love animals, you know. I'll help you with your dogs. Don't worry, I'll do most of the necessary for the animals in your paddocks. And if Peggy's feeling bad I'll prepare food for Sir James, and for you too, Olive. I haven't forgotten the household routine, and I'm not so against soiling my hands with menial tasks as some nurses are. We'll cope between us, I'm sure.'

'And I'm sure,' Olive replied, 'that I can't thank you enough. You'll have to imagine how wonderful for me it is to have sent out my SOS yesterday and to have you with us today.'

Angela wound up their confabulation by saying: 'One thing I will do if I can, my girl, is to get you looking a little more rounded. I'll feed you up and see you sleep at night and all that sort of thing, and make a new woman of you if you'll let me.'

They laughed together and carried Angela's several suitcases indoors and upstairs to the spare room she had occupied before.

Half an hour later Angela came downstairs to be reintroduced to her patient. Olive was again waiting for her, and had a chance to study her as they smiled up and down at each other. Angela was thirty-nine, she had said, and looked younger, no doubt because of her thick naturally blonde hair cut fairly short and the fringe that overhung her bright blue eyes. She had long white teeth, a ready smile and a sturdy figure that was also seductive. Her calves were muscled but her ankles were neat.

Her workwear was suitable – no nurse's uniform – well-fitting flowered shirt and skirt of darker material, tights and slip-on shoes. The only jewellery was a signet ring on the little finger of her right hand. Her make-up was discreet, a touch of mascara and a suspicion of lipstick on her shapely lips.

Olive led her into the study. Introductions were not required. Angela did all the talking.

'Well, Sir James, here I am again – the bad penny – you can't get rid of me. No, sir, no, don't you get up, please – you give me your hand – there – I'm kissing it better. Now what have you been up to? Oh, I know you've had your sadness, but grief's a good thing, and life has to go on, sweet life, especially when time's on the short side. I'll be crying along with you, but we'll have a laugh together too, I promise you that. And I must tell you before I'll let you say a single word, I must, Sir James, that I threw my cap in the air when your Olive rang me up and asked me to lend a hand. You and your wife, and your daughter who's my friend already, made such a great impression on me when I made your acquaintance. That's the honest truth. Now, first things last, if you'll pardon the Irishism, I solemnly promise not to be a chatterbox, I won't be a bore to you in that way, it's just that I'm excited to be back in The Old Hundred, and don't want you to have to make polite conversation to me. That's all! Tell me what you'd like me to do for you and don't try to spare my feelings, I'm ready and willing to obey.'

Olive wished she had been able to cosset her father in a manner half as uninhibited as Angela's.

The clever nursing of James Crighton did not stop on that first afternoon in his study. Angela was State Registered, but not bound by any of the starchier conventions of her profession, and she fitted in with his routine and respected his privacy and still managed to care for and make him comfortable on an almost twenty-four hour basis.

She had a bell rigged up between his dressing-room where he slept and the bedroom she slept in, actually Veronica's bedroom next door – James and Olive had stretched various points to allow Angela to occupy that room, and convenience settled the matter. She took over from Olive the preparation of his evening meal – Peggy only cooked lunch – and whetted his appetite with her specialities, Welsh Rarebit, tuna sandwiches, fruit salad with sweet liqueur, banana split. She was as good as her word and not too verbose – her voice was quiet, but always had an upward encouraging inflection. She had apparently inexhaustible patience and energy.

On the day after her arrival Olive heard her say to James: 'You've got me all to yourself this time round,' and she realised that her father was already, and would be, happier because he had never had his wife or his daughter – or any other woman – all to himself.

From then on, Olive was content to leave her father in Angela's care and return to the work she loved.

Angela's caring extended to Olive. She would have a rather more proper breakfast ready for Olive than used to be the case. She was sufficiently conscientious to be allowed to walk

Olive's dogs and to feed them, if their mistress overslept or was detained at the Surgery. She fed the animals in the paddocks on most days, as she had said she would.

In the evening, when Olive returned, there was hot food waiting for her to eat; and often, after Angela had taken her patient upstairs and tucked him in his bed, she would leave his door open and come downstairs for a cup of coffee and a chat with Olive – she declined to listen to music, during which she would be unable to hear a cry for help, although she said she was interested in opera.

Her chatting was confidential, she seemed to be determined to entrust Olive with secrets. For instance she established that she would take Sunday off, and told Olive what she did on those days, and why.

'I go to Bath, I've got a friend there, we meet – you know what men are, they can't be trusted for more than six days at a time, if that.'

Olive nodded knowledgeably, but had not understood.

'Guess where we spend the day? I'll give you a clue, and a bit more besides. We spend it in bed. He doesn't have much to offer another woman after I've finished with him. And it stops me getting itchy.'

Olive was intrigued by such revelations in spite of herself.

'Is he your lover?' she asked.

Angela laughed and replied: 'Do you want me to draw a map? Yes, you'd call him my lover. I call him my fancy man and an occasional roof over my head.'

'Do you lodge with him? Is he your lodging in Bath?'

'Don't you shout that from the rooftops! Your father might be shocked. I stay there when I've nowhere better to lay my head – and my body. He's not my husband or anything.'

'What's his name?'

'That's it – What's-his-name – let's leave it there, shall we?'

One day Angela inquired: 'Wouldn't you like to have friends in one of these days? I'd cook a meal for you and them, and it'd be fun for a change.'

'I haven't got many friends, none really, apart from Tim and the others I work with.'

'Is Tim married?'

'Oh yes, he and Helen have four children.'

'Don't you have a soft spot for any of those lusty young vets who kept your job warm?'

'They wouldn't fit in here.'

'What a lot of catching up ahead of you, love! What about that solicitor fellow, Martin?'

'I don't know anything about Martin. He isn't exactly my solicitor, he's the family one.'

'But he's been a help to you, you've told me he has.'

'That's different, it was business.'

'There's only one sort of business between a young man and a young woman.'

'No, you're wrong, it's not like that with me.'

'Oh well, I like you whatever you are like.'

On another evening Angela remarked: 'I thought such a lot of your mother. She was the most polite lady I've had dealings with. No wonder everybody's still mourning her! My child won't shed too many tears over me.'

'Your child?' Olive queried.

'Oh yes, half mine.'

'He or she, and how old?'

'He, and getting on for eighteen – a great big bad boy, Peter is, these days.'

'Where is he? You've never spoken about him before.'

'He's not my favourite topic of conversation. He was a slip-up when I was almost as innocent as you are. He lives with his father and step-mother.'

'Not What's-his-name?'

'Oh no, his father lives up north. I don't see Peter often, I haven't seen him for two years – or is it three? Talk about fitting in, how could I fit him into my way of earning my living?'

'Are you sad not to see him, Angela?'

'Not particularly. Let's change the subject.'

After a fortnight or so Olive thanked Angela as follows.

'You've made such a difference to my life. Daddy's much better than he was, I believe he's looking better than he ever did. I can't tell you how grateful I am.'

Angela responded with one of her clever humorous little squibs: 'You've pinched my speech, you naughty thing!'

One day Olive, having driven home for lunch

cooked by Peggy, was preparing food for Buddy and Whisper and passed the remark: 'My dogs aren't so hungry as usual, and I've an idea they've put on weight. What do you think?'

Angela, who had been watching and talking to her, replied: 'There's nothing wrong with them that I can see.'

'I'm afraid somebody must be giving them tit-bits.'

'Are you accusing me, Olive?'

'Good heavens, no! Of course not. It could be somebody in the village.'

'I don't like to be suspected. I know quite as well as you that dogs have their meals and no snacking ever.'

'Please – you're misunderstanding me – I haven't suspected you – please don't be cross!'

'I prefer to keep things crystal clear.'

'So do I – forgive me!'

The fact remained that Buddy and Whisper were in the kitchen when Angela cooked in the evenings, but stayed out of it while Peggy and Olive were cooking.

3

There was another small rough patch in the smooth development of the friendship between Olive and Angela, again relating to pets.

Angela sided with Denis over the ponies and sheep. She told Olive more forcefully than he already had that two of the five ponies, Moonbeam and Sunshine, were past praying for, that the sheep were on the verge of senility, good for nothing, and that to give them permission to die natural deaths was going to cost a small fortune in vet's bills.

'You know more about vets' fees than I do, but an outsider can't help seeing what you may not have noticed – a cull is plainly indicated, love, and personally I'd say the whole menagerie's expendable.'

Olive did not like it, that is to be bossed about, and be taught lessons in animal welfare, of which she had professional knowledge. Besides, her sheep were called Eeny, Meeny, Miny, Mo and Tina, her mother had given them to her when they were lambs, and she had ridden Moonbeam and Sunshine in the old days. They were all her pets, if not so dear to her as the dogs, and while Denis was looking after them, and expenses that might be incurred were not her concern, the idea of curtailing their future never crossed her mind. But times had changed, and she could not dismiss Angela's opinion logically.

'What would happen to my sheep?' she asked. 'I won't have them put down.'

'Denis says a farmer friend of his has some hill land and would let them graze there undisturbed.'

'Do you think that's true?'

'Why worry? The thing I know for certain is that I'm sorry and all that, but I don't want any more to do with them – they're such smelly old things. And they're going to be too much of a burden for you, what with your work and your father unwell.'

'I suppose I could ask Tim over to examine my ponies.'

'That's right – and please, sweetie, for your own sake, don't be sentimental and land yourself in a bad mess later on.'

She agreed. She permitted Angela to oversee the dark deed. One evening she returned to find only one pony, Trix, who was relatively fit, in the Old Hundred paddocks.

She shed a few tears. Angela was bracing to the point of callousness, although she promised to continue to do odd jobs for Trix. Olive had to admit that she was relieved to be rid of her sweet encumbrances.

These differences between herself and Angela were a small price to pay, first for their association, so intriguing and educative for the younger woman, and secondly for the magic wand that was being waved on a daily basis over her father. She forgave even if she could not altogether forget, and decided that she herself might have been more at fault than the other way round.

James' recovery, psychological and physical, was due to Angela's attentions. She boosted his confidence with her flattery and flirting, and challenged him to exert himself and get his blood and his muscles to move more freely.

Her 'bossiness', her 'bullying' of her patient, had a rough charm as well as medical efficacy.

'Prepare yourself, Sir James, I'm going to drag you out of doors by your grey hairs... Stir those stumps, Sir Knight, and arm me in to dinner!'

She forced him to help her with crosswords, to read to her while she sewed on his many missing buttons, to watch TV programmes she chose, and to use his mind to try to entertain her.

She took him shopping in Bath, and got him out of tweed jackets, trousers with braces and heavy brogues and into all-weather tracksuits and trainers. She sometimes pleaded indisposition so that he had to think of her wellbeing instead of concentrating on his own. She was infinitely resourceful. She drove him to see the lions of Longleat and to look at the Crescents of Bath, and dragged him protesting into Wookey Hole. One afternoon she took him to see a movie in Bath.

He thanked Olive for finding him a treasure. He said artlessly to the daughter of his wife that he had not had such fun since he was a boy. He hurt Olive's feelings, or would have hurt them if she had been less altruistic, by not only raving about Angela as he never raved about Veronica, but also by seeming to establish a closer tie to his nurse than was ever established with herself. One day he took Olive aside, metaphorically, and asked her not to bother Angela by making her listen to operas – 'She doesn't understand that stuff any more than I do, and I don't want her to be bored. Don't drive her away, darling, will you?'

One day Angela put a different question to Olive: 'I hope you think I'm doing right by your father?'

'Indeed I do,' Olive replied. 'He's improved in every way.'

'You don't mind my teasing him?'

'No – he enjoys it – and that's the object of the exercise.'

'You wouldn't like me to pack my bags?'

'Definitely not, Angela! You mustn't think of leaving us. I want you to stay for as long as the money holds out.'

'Oh well – that's nice – but I'm not expecting to be a fixture.'

'And I wish you were one.'

A subsequent snatch of conversation with her father caused Olive momentary concern.

He called her into his study on a spring morning and said to her: 'Something odd's happening, my dear, and I feel I should bring it to your notice.'

'Are you ill, Daddy?'

'No, on the contrary, I'm unusually well on this beautiful day. No – but I have a confession to make – it's about the very last thing I expected, and I'm sure the same will apply to you – I seem to be falling in love. I'm sorry but there it is.'

'Love with Angela?'

'Exactly.'

'Oh Daddy...'

'I apologise because I know it's only two and a half months since your mother died. But I don't believe she could be objecting to my finding a little happiness before the sun goes down, and I'm hoping you'll soon take the same view. I'm not planning to alter anything that could affect you, darling, and I'm too old to be rash. That's the whole story.'

'Does Angela know how you feel for her?'

'She's a sensible woman, and is kind enough to indulge an old man's fancy. I haven't exactly declared myself, if that's the right way to put it.'

'I suppose I should congratulate you.'

'No need for that. You're not too shocked?'

'Oh Daddy!'

Olive brushed these exchanges into the back of her mind. She had heard of men of her father's age getting crushes on stray women. She was fairly sure she could stop him being sillier than he had so far been, if necessary.

Unfortunately James caught a spring cold, the clinging type of infection, and bronchitis ensued.

He began to run a high temperature, Angela sat up with him for two nights, and Olive suggested employment of another nurse.

Angela had a better idea.

'Don't – you'll have to pay through the nose for a night-nurse from an agency – I can cope, or I could, if you'd give me permission to move him into the other side of the big bed I've been sleeping in. I could then get more rest than I do in a chair, and still be aware of a crisis. Would it be wrong, love, would it upset you, would it upset your father, if we shared your parents' matrimonial bed?'

Olive said no, meaning that she would grin and bear it.

Her father began to recover and to convalesce, and she found it more upsetting that he did not move back into the bed in his dressing-room. But what was she to say? She could think of no way to object that would not sound prim or presumptuous.

Gratitude restrained her – Angela had saved her father's life and her family money. Gratitude posed a different problem: how was Angela to be rewarded for what she had done, her kindness beyond the call of duty, or in more mundane terms her overtime?

Olive broached the subject to her father one evening, when he was back in his study and Angela was cooking in the kitchen.

'Daddy, I'm sorry to bother you but I need your advice.'

'What is it?' he answered with a new sharp

edge to his voice. Olive had noticed since he was ill that he spoke to her less gently and fondly than he used to.

'It's about Angela.'

'I hope there's no ill feeling between you.'

'No – why should there be? Why do you ask?'

'You know I don't want to lose her.'

'Yes – of course – nor do I – and I need your advice about how to keep her happy.'

'Is she not happy? Has she said she isn't happy?'

'No, Daddy – please let me finish what I started to say! I think we owe her for saving your life, and I've been wondering what we could give her.'

'Olive, I was hoping I could leave the whole question of remuneration to you – I don't feel up to money matters, and it would be an embarrassment for me to be paying Angela while she nursed me so caringly.'

'Does that mean you think we should pay her more? We've become such friends that I was thinking a present of some kind might be more suitable, more acceptable.'

'It should be money – she's saving to buy a house for herself and her son.'

'Oh? How much money, do you think?'

'She worked at least twice as hard, twenty-four hours a day – pay her accordingly.'

'Twice her weekly pay? But that'd be an awful lot – that could be what an agency nurse would charge, and Angela stopped me getting in an agency nurse for that very reason.'

'You asked for advice, my dear, and I've given it to you.'

'For how long should I pay her twice the pay we all agreed?'

'Until further notice.'

'The money you gave me will run out.'

'That remains to be seen. My age and the state of my health will doubtless settle the question to your satisfaction.'

'Daddy, really! You're being very hard on me. You ought to remember that I've done nothing except to put you first and try to help you.'

'There are difficulties for me that you don't appreciate, darling Olive. I apologise for speaking roughly. My hope has been that you would extricate me from a practical dilemma. I'll support whatever you decide to do in respect of the money.'

'You're talking in riddles, Daddy. Are you in any trouble?'

'I'm far out of range of the trouble you may have in mind. No, my dear, it's good luck not bad luck that troubles me. Excuse my grumpiness, if you will.'

Olive's stressful reaction to this conversation was not alleviated by her subsequent talk with Angela after supper and after James had been put to bed on that same evening.

She began by offering the extra money tentatively, expecting it to be refused and that she might be giving offence into the bargain.

Angela surprised her by accepting it quite casually.

'It'll come in handy,' she said. 'I'm a spend-thrift and Peter's my luxury, we're always skint, so three cheers for the Crightons.' Her inhibitions about costing them too much seemed to have been shed completely.

Olive said: 'I was thinking it would add to your savings for this house I hear you're going to buy.'

'That too.'

'Angela, what do you make of my father's health now?'

'He's blooming, isn't he?'

'Well, earlier, when I spoke to him, he was irritable and said incomprehensible things.'

'What sort of things?'

'That he had a dilemma, and it was to do with luck. Are you the dilemma?'

'Not to notice – don't you pay attention – he gets worked up over me – but it's what keeps him going in my opinion.'

'How am I supposed to extricate him from this dilemma?'

'He doesn't want business to come between him and me, he wants you to do the dirty work.'

'You won't let him go farther than he should, will you?'

'Oh Olive, what a worrier you are! I check his temperature and blood pressure until we're sick of it. He's fine. I've got him off the pills Dr Wood put him on, pills for blood pressure and digestion and water, but I can get him on again from one minute to the next. I'm proud of introducing a twinkle into his old eye, and no harm done. There! You leave him to me, and sleep tight!'

The next private conversation between Olive and her father was unimaginably worse.

It again occurred in his study in the evening, on a Monday not long enough after the death of Veronica Crighton. He summoned Olive this time, and seated her formally in the armchair facing him – they were on either side of the fireplace – it was April and the fire was unlit.

'My dear Olive, I have finally resolved the difficulties I mentioned to you a little while ago. In a word, they boil down to the truth – the truth and whether and how I should tell it. My resolution is simply that it has to be told, told to you without delay. And I must beg you to treat it with your characteristic compassion and sweetness.'

'Heavens, Daddy! Please don't beat about the bush, I hate suspense.'

'I was not happy with your Mother. I never was, we shouldn't have married, we were oil and water, and I'm afraid I made her as unhappy as, looking back, she made me.'

'Are you hinting that you're more involved with Angela?'

'Please don't rush me. I'm not hinting anything, I'll make myself clear if you're patient. Of course I was the gainer from marrying Veronica, from her kindness in marrying me – I became the lord of her manor of Luffield, and resided at The Old Hundred. And then you arrived on the

scene, and you were the reward and the justifica-
tion of our marriage. Sentiment apart, you were
the only representative of the younger generation
of both your mother's family and my own. I
loved her for bearing my child, and perhaps she
loved me for siring you, but we didn't make
each other happy.'

'Oh Daddy, I wish...'

'No, Olive, you must listen – I've been listened to by everybody except my wife and my
daughter – and now I must be allowed to have
my say. Happiness was a closed book for me, all
I knew was how to be busy, and that's the story
of my life, the story up to now.'

'Oh no,' Olive groaned, but her father either
did not or would not hear.

'Now I'm going to take the risk of your
laughing at me or crying. I've fallen in love for
the first time at this eleventh and perhaps almost
twelfth hour, and the only unhappy aspect of
my love for Angela is that we cannot have long
to be together. I'm about to ask her to marry me
– as you would prefer me not to beat about the
bush, I state the nub of the matter without
more ado. I have now shared a bed with the
lady and contracted obligations, and again it's
right that I should warn you, darling Olive, that
I'm not to be deflected from my plan. As for
second thoughts, there is not the slightest chance
of my having any. I'm sorry if I've saddened
you, although I'm sure you would want me to
be happy at all costs.'

'Oh dear! I'm sorry that I'm speechless, Daddy.'

'You won't suffer materially, Olive.'

'I don't care about material things.'

'Probably I should have been more explanatory when we last had a chinwag. I should have explained that my difficulties related to paying the woman I hoped to marry. My dilemma was whether to act as her employer or her suitor, and I was short with you for not leaving me out of the financial reckoning. Anyway, the dilemma will be superseded if Angela agrees to be my wife.'

'True.'

'I don't expect your blessing, my dear, but I hope you won't raise objections which would cast a shadow and complicate our future life together. Angela's extremely fond of you, and I understand that you reciprocate her feelings, and the ideal would obviously be to change nothing and carry on almost as we do at present.'

'Daddy, can I have time to digest all this information?'

'Of course, on the understanding that I'm naturally in a hurry.'

'Oh well – I'm not standing in your way, if you've really made up your mind. Can I just ask you not to be too hasty?'

He shrugged his shoulders, frowning. He was very excited, his face was flushed and his eyes behind his spectacles seemed to glitter.

Olive stood up and crossed over to kiss him on the forehead.

'Daddy,' she began, hesitated, and concluded: 'I wish you well.'

'Thank you, dear Olive.'

She left the room. She went into the kitchen and told Angela she had a headache and would be skipping supper. She went upstairs, cried a bit, and worried over what on earth she should do next.

In time she heard her father and Angela coming upstairs – it was nine-thirty, his bedtime. Half an hour later Angela descended the stairs to tidy the kitchen and have her customary cigarette and cup of tea.

Olive followed her down and, standing in the doorway, asked: 'Has Daddy proposed to you?'

'What's that? Are you joking?'

'He says he's going to.'

'Bless him! The man could be my grandfather – I'm not vain, but I hope I'll be able to improve on his offer. How are you, Olive – headache better?'

'It's not bad.'

'Have a cup of tea.'

'Thank you. Angela, has he really not talked about marrying you?'

'Oh, he rambles on, half the time he's talking in his sleep – I take no notice when I'm not wide awake. Gentlemen his age feel free to say terrible things to their nurses, you know. Has he been getting you into a fret? Forget it, Olive – I'll keep you posted of proposals I receive from any quarter. Sit down and drink your tea, and I'll tell you tales that I mean to put in a book one day – *A Nurse's Bedtime Stories*, I'll call it.'

* * *

Twenty-four hours later, on the Tuesday evening of the same week, again in the kitchen round about ten o'clock, Angela, having lit her cigarette, said to Olive: 'He's popped it.'

'When?'

'A quarter of an hour ago. He was in bed by then. I asked him if he was going to jump out and kneel at my feet.'

'He couldn't do that.'

'Precisely. I said I'd marry him when he could get down on his knees and get up again unaided.'

'Oh Angela!'

'I couldn't take him seriously. I made him laugh in the end, though he's not too strong in the humour department.'

'Poor Daddy!'

'Don't you be too kind to him, Olive. He's still strong and selfish, like other men.'

'Well, I'd rather you didn't marry him, I must say that, not so soon after my mother died, but I wouldn't want to ruin your chances.'

'What chances? For pity's sake! I have some pride left in me.'

On the Wednesday, as usual, Olive departed without seeing her father. She did not return from the Surgery at lunchtime – Angela could feed her dogs; in the evening she walked Buddy and Whisper for an hour in the spring weather; she therefore did not see her father until suppertime, when she was afraid he looked shifty – but he was shaky, too, and abstracted.

On Thursday it was the same routine, up to the point when she parked her Fiesta round in the old farmyard and entered the house.

Angela was waiting for her in the kitchen. Her clothes, her hair, gave the game away. She wore a smart pale blue silk dress with an orchid pinned to her bosom, and her blonde hair was up on top of her head.

She held out her arms to Olive, smiling uneasily, laughing ruefully, and said: 'Prepare to be hugged by your stepmother!'

'You haven't!' Olive replied.

'He forced me. He's been on at me for ever since we talked on Monday. What's the difference? But I'm not too pleased with the way he looks. You'd better go and see what you think, and if we should call out Dr Wood. He had the whole thing fixed up, Olive, the Register Office and goodness knows what else, and in the end I was too tired to say no, no, no yet again. But we may have to take special care of him after all the excitement.'

Olive duly congratulated her father as he rested in his nuptial couch on his second wedding day. His flush was 'hectic', in medical parlance, and his forehead glistened with perspiration. His remaining grey hairs were also damp, and the hand he held out to her was at once wet and cold.

'Are you feeling okay, Daddy?'

He ignored her question and said: 'Do me a favour, Olive, go down to the cellar and fetch a bottle of the Veuve Clicquot champagne – there should be three bottles left – I meant to deal with it myself.'

He lay back and closed his eyes.

'Daddy, would you like to see Dr Wood?'

'No – I'll be down to supper in ten minutes – just do as I say and ask Angela to come and be with me.'

Olive obeyed orders. An hour later Angela helped James in his dressing-gown downstairs. He insisted on champagne and toasts were drunk, Olive toasted the newly-weds as requested, and James drank a toast to Angela, then he dropped his glass and began to cry. Angela supported him back to the stairs and slowly up them one at a time, while he blubbed repeatedly: 'Don't get a doctor – I've tried to be fair to both of you – I won't see a doctor – I've done my best.'

At about nine-thirty Angela joined Olive and explained: 'He wanted no food, and now he's asleep, thank goodness. Oh Olive, I shouldn't have done it, I haven't been a good nurse, but I meant well. No, no, I couldn't eat anything either – we had a proper lunch at any rate. I can't stay with you, I'll go back in case he wakes.'

At eleven o'clock Olive retired to bed and slept – she had had a long busy day and tiredness took precedence over shock, anxiety and apprehensiveness.

She was woken between two and three o'clock by Angela bursting in to her bedroom, crying, 'He's gone, he's gone!'

James had died almost in his sleep, Angela related – he had woken and groaned, then the life ebbed out of him in a rush. It was a mercy, he had not suffered, and he thought he was happy, his last words were that he was happy, for he had done as he wished – she had made his wish come true, even if it had been the death of him.

Olive comforted her, and the small hours of morning passed.

Early the next day the daughter and the widow split the tasks that had to be done. Olive rang Tim Spell and Martin East and broke the news to Peggy and Denis. Angela rang undertakers and arranged to meet the vicar of Luffield and Barstone, the Reverend Walters.

Martin East undertook to inform the local press, when he had recovered from the surprise of hearing about the remarriage. He said he would dig out Sir James' will and come over to see Olive in a day or two. Eventually she was able to take Buddy and Whisper for their walk. When she returned she found two messages, one from Angela to say she had gone to see Mr Walters, the other from Peggy asking her to telephone Mr Martin East urgently.

She did so.

Martin said: 'Your father made a more recent will. He didn't come to us, he used a firm in Bath, Harris and Hurst, and the will was apparently signed and witnessed after the wedding yesterday. Mr Harris rang me half an hour ago, everything seems to be in order, but this new will negates and nullifies the one held here at Tyndall and East. I'm awfully sorry, Olive.'

'What's in it, do you know?'

'I know more or less.'

'Has he left The Old Hundred to Angela?'

'No – not so bad – he's left her the money that he apparently claims was his own – enough to buy or build a house, I understand – but he also grants her an entitlement to live in your house for as long as she pleases – which would explain why he didn't ask us to prepare such a document.'

'Why, Martin?'

'I couldn't have sanctioned the latter clause while I was acting for yourself and in your interests as well as for your father.'

'Oh well! By the way, how did Mr Harris know of my father's death?'

'Lady Crighton informed him.'

The funeral was quieter than some. The few neighbours in the congregation were those who had managed to break through Olive's barriers and strike up feeble friendships with her; the rest, the residue of the guests who had dined at The Old Hundred in Veronica's days, stayed away to show disapproval of the nurse who had sandbagged Sir James almost at death's door and carted him off to the Register Office. Only two or three of his former constituents turned up. The people of Luffield and others in the locality attended partly for Olive's sake, partly to take a peep at her stepmother. Solicitors, vets and tradespeople filled one or two of the otherwise empty pews.

After considerable discussion, James was not buried in his first wife's grave, as he had planned many years ago, but cremated, and his ashes were scattered at the farthest end of The Old Hundred garden.

It was also agreed that Martin East, not Mr Harris, whose connection with the family began and ended with the will he had drafted, should help Olive to sort out her father's desk, files, accumulation of papers, bank accounts and so on. Angela took some of James' clothes for her son Peter, but Martin carried away for charity shops and for disposal several black bags-full.

For the week following the funeral Olive stayed at home with Angela.

The suspicions that might have done damage to their relationship were allayed by Angela's frankness and recognition of problematic areas.

She apologised to Olive until the latter was forced to say seemingly heartless things. For instance, when Angela said she was sad to have robbed Olive of her beloved Daddy, Olive replied that her father had not been so beloved as he probably deserved to be, and they had had nothing in common except some of the blood in their veins.

Again, when Angela said, 'My father died when I was ten years old – I'd give anything to have known him better than I did,' Olive retorted, 'Well, I didn't know my father in any real sense, and he didn't begin to know me, and I can't pretend to be sorry.'

On another tack Angela explained: 'James

made me swear on the head of my son Peter not to tell you what he was up to. He thought you'd be against it.'

'I might not have been. If it was more … more above board, I might have been in favour.'

'He thought you'd be upset anyway.'

'Well, yes, he was right.'

'I know, I know I should have told you and consulted you – don't rub salt in my wounds, sweetie. The only thing I can't blame myself for is the money.'

'How much money did he leave you?'

'Oh I don't care, I'm no good at figures, what's important is that I made it crystal clear that I would never accept a single penny of the money that was your birthright through your mother.'

'Did you discuss his new will with him?'

'Only to that extent. There was obviously a difference between your inheritance from your mother and your inheritance from your father. I thought he could do what he liked with money he had made, money that wasn't exactly family money. I've prided myself on taking nothing that isn't mine from you. But now I can see in your face that you think I've not been honest. Listen, I'll return my bequest to you as soon as I receive it – I don't want any slightest crime on my conscience.'

'For heaven's sake, Angela, please don't talk about crimes!'

'But you gave me quite a dirty look.'

'I didn't, I wouldn't, I promise you.'

'I'll return my bequest anyway.'

'You know I won't agree to that, Angela.'

'We'll see.'

'No, we won't, that's definite. Tell me, how did Daddy know those other solicitors?'

'I expect he'd done business with them before.'

'He didn't deal with Bath firms – we never knew business people in Bath, for us it was either Warminster or Bristol.'

'Oh well, ask me another! I had nothing whatsoever to do with Harris and Hurst.'

'You rang them the morning after he died, and they informed Martin East of the new will.'

'Certainly I did, I couldn't let Martin come over here and give you a load of misleading information – it would have been cruel, to let one solicitor raise your hopes and another dash them – I couldn't allow it. Luckily I had heard James arranging his will on the telephone – I remembered the name of the firm and obtained their telephone number from Directory Enquiries.'

'I see,' Olive commented, or rather Olive fibbed, for a tiny interior voice whispered that Angela was running rings around her.

One day she turned their talk in a more personal direction.

'Did Daddy know about What's-his-name?'

'Certainly not.'

'Would you have gone on meeting What's-his-name after you were Daddy's wife?'

'I might. I expect I would. Don't look prissy, love! You're an old-fashioned girl, you haven't logged on to post-pill morality – we're no more chaste nowadays than the boys have ever been. And there's an old-fashioned saying that ought to set your mind at rest – "What the eye doesn't see the heart doesn't grieve over." I wasn't planning to betray your father publicly or run off with his dosh.'

'Did sex figure in the courtship – while you were in the same bed?'

'That's not a prissy question.'

'I have wondered.'

'Yes and no. He liked to play around a bit, and I'm not all that particular. He was welcome, and it was friendly and fine so long as it was harmless. Besides, What's-his-name's acting hard to get at present, and, though I can be forgetful short term, by nature I'm the female equivalent of a ladies' man – something's better than nowt.'

'Daddy felt obliged to marry you because of the double bed.'

'He needn't have – no possibility of a baby.'

'He was even more old-fashioned than me.'

Repeatedly Angela returned to the other clause of James' will that affected Olive: 'If I do hang on to my bequest, I'll use it to buy my house, so I won't be your lodger for long. Meanwhile, until I go, I'll care for you, I'll be your carer, and won't be a troublesome tenant, cross my heart. Peter's longing for us to live together again – he's so grateful to you and your father for all you've done for me and are doing for the two of us. Thank you, thank you, dear Olive!'

Hugs and kisses resembled the punctuation of these conversations, the ambiguous dots and dashes, and the obstructive full stops.

4

Martin East informed Olive that her father had left one hundred and fifty thousand pounds to his second wife, a sum sufficient to buy a small property.

As a result, Olive's net financial resources would just enable her to live in and maintain the fabric of The Old Hundred for the foreseeable future. His opinion of the right of residence conferred upon Angela was that it could and probably should be challenged. He explained that it amounted to an open-ended invitation to share her home – and not only residentially, for the one right exercised for several years might well confer another, the right in effect to own a percentage of the property.

'Oh but that will never happen,' Olive said.

'Are you speaking emotionally or legally?' Martin queried.

'I do know that I don't know the law, but Angela's my friend, she's given me assurances that she won't be here for long, and I trust her never to try to steal anything from me.'

'Necessity's such a devil, Olive – come and sit in my office one day, you'll be amazed by how badly good people can behave when they're threatened or if they're greedy. Angela has a long life-expectancy, and you've been friends with her for a short time.'

'But you've only met her once or twice. Don't you like her?'

'It's nothing personal – I'm considering your welfare, and being as professional as I can be.'

'What do you mean by "challenge"?'

'A court case, I'm afraid.'

'That's out of the question. I could never sue Angela, who was so good to my father – she even married him with the best of intentions. For that matter I can't imagine myself disregarding my father's wish. And I'm sure you'll understand when you know Angela better.'

Martin devoted three working days ostensibly to clearing up after James Crighton and explaining the responsibilities that had devolved on Olive; he therefore lunched at The Old Hundred with his client and her stepmother.

Olive had been unsettled by Martin's cautious references to Angela, and was now embarrassed by Angela's lack of caution.

Angela described him as a 'dish': 'What a dish!' Olive had never liked Angela's coarser terminology, and was displeased that Martin should be compared to a square meal. 'He looks handsomer every time I catch his eye,' Angela said. 'I could create beautiful music with that man. He's not your private property, is he?'

'No – he's my solicitor.'

'I don't mind what he does, it's what he is that makes the embers glow.'

For Olive, this was a new way of thinking in general, and in particular almost ruinous of her relations with Martin. She suddenly saw that he was tall, dark, lithe, healthy, with a twinkle in his eye and very white teeth. She had been blind, she realised, and her ignorance of the opposite sex and of romance in action was rudely rammed home. The secondary consequence was that she became even shyer than usual, and lost the ease with which they had pored over papers together in her father's secluded study.

The lunches at which Martin and Angela met socially were not the success Olive had once hoped for. Angela's oncoming approaches were evidently – and thankfully – not to Martin's taste.

For instances, she asked him: 'Have you got a wife and six children at home? ... Unmarried at your age? – You must be quick on your feet! ... Still living at home with an aged p, fancy that! I'd have thought you'd be lonely in the evenings, not to speak of the nights... Well, if you're ever in need of a dancing partner, call on me – you know where you'll find me.'

Martin's responses were more like cross-questioning.

'I hear you have a son? ... And you're hoping to set up house together? ... Will you be resuming your career as a nurse? ... What are Peter's interests? What type of work will he be looking for?'

Olive was relieved when Martin said he

thought his task was done. She agreed rather reluctantly to his request for a moment's conversation on matters not directly relating to her father. They sat in the same chairs on either side of the fireplace in the study, where she had recently heard a declaration of love carried to matrimonial lengths.

'I've wondered if you'd come to tea one weekend day, and meet my mother. She's aged, as Angela puts it, but still clear-headed. She's heard of you, she knows the parents of Tim Spell, and she'd very much like to make your acquaintance.' Martin continued: 'I hope I'm not speaking out of turn.'

'No,' she replied in a voice she feared was strangulated.

'Would you come to tea?'

'Not yet, Martin.'

'One day, though?'

'Yes, if you ask me.'

'Thank you. I will. And please do remember that if you're in difficulties of any description, ring me – my calls are transferred to my home after working hours, so I'm always available.'

'My turn to thank you – thank you for all your help.'

'It's been a pleasure. Oh – one last thing, which I thought I should pass on. I made a few inquiries about Mr Harris, the solicitor your father instructed when he didn't instruct Tyndall and East. Mr and Mrs Harris have a big house in Lansdowne and let out rooms to nurses – they have connections with hospitals, nursing homes and agencies. Angela may stay there between engagements, and if so she would have told your father where he could have his will done without being asked any awkward questions.'

Olive was not sceptical or suspicious. She did not mentally record everything said to her that might be of use or incriminating at some later stage. She was trusting – her head was, or seemed to be, in the clouds, where love held sway to the strains of operatic music.

She could not be sure that Angela had lied to her. She could not believe Angela was a liar. Had Angela meant that she had had no dealings of a legal kind with Harris and Hurst? She had perhaps never meant to convey an impression that she was unacquainted with one or either or both.

The same ambiguity applied to other claims she had made. Was part of her charm its trickery? Had she at least fibbed about feeding forbidden titbits to the dogs? Had she forged her own wedding ring?

Olive could not remember accurately enough, she was not disposed to dredge up incidents and items better forgotten, she swallowed hard and decided to look ahead and judge the future on its merits. Yet a trail of low cloud or fog, which would metaphorically qualify as a 'sea fret', drifted across the friendship of stepdaughter and stepmother, and Olive was increasingly anxious to get out of the house and back to work.

She broached that subject to Angela.

'Would you be all right if I was away every weekday, and you were here alone?'

'Don't worry, love – I'll give the house a spring clean – my hands won't be idle, so the devil can't catch hold of them. You follow your calling to nurse animals – it's the call of the wild.'

'Would it be a bore for you to see to Trix and feed Buddy and Whisper at lunchtime?'

'You're not worried about my feeding your dogs?'

'No – it was only overfeeding them that worried me.'

'I know, sweetie. I wouldn't dare. Don't you bother to drive home in the middle of the day – I'll look after things. And I'll cook you a hot meal in the evenings.'

Olive's mind was not completely set at rest by this snatch of conversation: what might Angela find while spring cleaning? And would Peggy be willing to cook lunch only for her?

But she shrugged her shoulders in response to the first question – who cared if Angela read private correspondence between the elder Crightons? – and after all Peggy, and Denis too, had reasons to be civil to their new ladyship: Olive had written out sizeable cheques for each of them, and she and Angela together had made the presentations, pretending they were legacies from the late master.

Olive duly returned to the Surgery, and Angela was as good as her word in respect of supper, which they ate in the kitchen.

Their conversations now ranged farther afield. Angela revealed that she was born and brought up in the village of Carslow in Derbyshire. Her father died when she was ten, he had been a rough lot, whereas her mother was a teacher and had gone back to teaching to support herself and her two children, Angela and her brother Cliff – Cliff with whom her family lost touch. Was her mother alive? No, she died of overwork when Angela was sixteen – 'She was my guardian angel – naughty persons with tails got at me when she was gone.' Peter had been conceived in Derbyshire. Had she loved Peter's father? 'Oh yes – but oh no in your lingo, sweetie – nothing polite about it!'

Angela was no longer taking Sunday off. She had refused to accept wages from Olive, she accepted money only for housekeeping expenses – she had some savings for personal expenditure, and her bequest to look forward to, but said she was being 'careful' for Peter's sake. Anyway, since What's-his-name had vanished, she could not be fagged to leave The Old Hundred to tussle with the tourists in Bath.

The side effect of her confinement under Olive's roof, notwithstanding that she was opting for it and never stopped saying she was in love with the house, was that she ran out of jobs to do, accumulated excess energy, grew restive, and was apt verbally to stroll down memory lane – love lane, more precisely – in the evenings.

She described the loss of her virginity in some detail – in an uncomfortable position in the

65

backyard of the house in Carslow. She clearly derived satisfaction from weaving a smutty spell over Olive, who was simultaneously attracted and repelled by the light thrown on the seamier side of life. To qualify as a nurse, take the exams and do the donkey work, she had lived on subsidies from her relations and presents from gentlemen friends. Men could be very grateful to nurses, who knew how to tickle their fancies, she revealed. Night duty was a gold mine, according to Angela, or it had been in her young hungry days. She referred to the contraceptive pill as a lifebuoy for poor girls with their way to make in the world – it was 'their means to private means'. Her fears in hospital were, first, of Matron, secondly that she would be the death of an over-enthusiastic patient in a secluded room.

Sometimes Olive asked her to stop – 'I don't want to hear all this stuff.'

'Don't be silly – we all do – it's the most popular topic, more popular than the weather – sit still and learn your ABC.'

Actually, Olive thought, it was more her XYZ than her ABC, for Angela told her things sophisticated, specialised, perverse and plain dangerous that had little connection with the natural expression of lust, let alone love. Erotic zones, in Angela's geography, existed in regions that Olive had thought were beyond the pale. She had enjoyed in principle, whether or not in practice, experiences regarded as more or less harsh punishments in polite society, getting herself spanked, even bound hand and foot and beaten.

'How horrible!' Olive exclaimed.

'It's an acquired taste, you lovely little babe in arms, that's what sex is – and you remember it when you grow up and entice Martin into your parlour. You play around, you experiment, and one day or night you'll see stars, even if you may be in the gutter.'

Inevitably, conversation was a wasting asset for a woman of Angela's disposition, and she began to complain that Luffield was dead.

'Your father died on me, or nearly on me, and Luffield snuffed it long long ago, and The Old Hundred's fine, a fine retirement home for distressed gentlewomen – but I need action in a hurry. Your father was past it, but at any rate he was male – I'll go berserk if I don't see a man in his socks and shirt tails before too long. Can't you find me a pair of trousers, Olive? What about inviting Martin over?'

Angela's own answer to these queries was to ask Olive if she could get Peter down to stay for a weekend.

'I haven't seen him for ages, I've no idea what he's up to, and he won't stay more than two or three days and he'd be better than nothing for me. Besides, there's such a lot of space in your house, it does seem a shame not to use a bit more of it.'

Olive had to agree in spite of her premonitions of disaster, and again the uneasy feeling that she was losing control of her life.

Perhaps, on the other hand, Peter would be the solution of problems, and would whisk Angela out of The Old Hundred and into a cottage made for two – Angela had said something about their house-hunting.

He was worse than Olive could have imagined – six feet tall, heavily built verging on obese, low forehead, spiky crewcut black hair, black frowning eyebrows, deep set black eyes, black bristly beard, unclean teeth with gaps and an insolent manner.

He was unbelievable, a monster out of a horror comic, but at least Olive was not alone in finding him so – Angela commented in an aside when she had brought him back from Warminster station, 'My God, what have I given birth to!' The mere sight of him frightened Peggy, and he began badly with Denis by calling him 'Grampa'.

He called his mother and Olive by diminutives of their Christian names, Angie and Ollie or Ol, and coupled them together as if they were more than friends; but his meanings were hard to fathom partly because he seemed to be unable to finish a word – he greeted Olive thus, 'Ni' pla' you go' 'ere, Ol' – and partly because his visage was expressionless.

His appetite for food and his greed were respectively exhausting and repulsive. Almost a week's consumption of potatoes by Olive and Angela was eaten in one meal by Peter, he gobbled a whole hand of bananas at a sitting, and snacked crisps and Mars Bars non-stop while he slumped in front of the TV set – his litter was everywhere. He was disgusting, he stunk out the house several times daily, and Peggy refused to make his bed after doing it twice – she said she could only have touched his sheets with pliers.

On the evening of his arrival Olive had tried to be a gracious hostess and introduced him to the dogs and to Trix and showed him round the house.

He said he liked puppy-dogs – maybe it was his redeeming feature, everybody is supposed to have one; but he patted Buddy too roughly, and lifted up Whisper, a demeaning experience for a hefty Ridgeback.

He was quite interested in Trix, and asked Olive: 'D' you ri' 'im?'

'She's a mare,' Olive explained.

'Wha's tha'?'

'She's female.'

'D' you ri' 'er?'

'I used to, but she's old now.'

'Looks a' ri'.'

'Well, she's not fit to be ridden.'

'She's goo' gir'.'

After the tour of the house Peter demanded: 'Where d'you play billiar's?'

'There isn't a billiard table.'

'Wha'? No billiar' table wi' so mu' loll' around?'

'I'm afraid I don't follow you.'

'You ge' in a billiar' table, tha's my advi'. Don' say you cou'nt affor' one.'

He stayed five days, not a weekend. Olive made a point of leaving earlier and returning later during his visit. She was not intolerant, and although she had a temper it was the slow, slow-burning type. But her gorge rose steadily as Peter offended her with his brutal manners and alarmed her with his crass unfriendliness, and as complaints from Peggy and Denis multiplied – he had raided the fruit cage, knocked the heads off flowers, frightened the goldfish in the lily pool somehow, and Peggy was infuriated by his thefts of food from her kitchen.

Moreover, Peter brought to a head Olive's less good feelings for his mother. Angela had nothing to tell Olive about a house she and Peter would consider moving into, and there was no mention of their moving out. James Crighton's will had been proved by now, and his money paid over to Angela, who made no sign of putting it to the purpose for which it was bequeathed. Olive, belatedly, began to entertain the idea that Angela was treating The Old Hundred as her home and might be difficult to dislodge.

It was in this smouldering state that Olive arrived back from work at seven-thirtyish on the fifth day of Peter's stay. As usual, she collected the dogs and went into the paddock to feed and water Trix. The pony's flanks had elongated bumps, weals, the unmistakeable weals caused by being whipped with a switch – probably the switch that always hung with coats in the down-stairs washroom.

She grew hot, seemed to boil, strode indoors, found Angela and Peter watching TV in the drawing-room, and accused the youth straight out: 'You've been whipping my pony. You cruel boy! Get out of my house, you're to leave my house instantly!'

Angela stood up, blushing and defensive, and Peter mumbled in his mother's direction, 'Wha' she say?'

Olive addressed Angela: 'He's been beating Trix.'

'Oh Olive!' She turned on Peter: 'Have you done that?'

' 'ere, Ange, keep yer wool on!'

'What have you done to the pony?'

'On'y went for a ri'.'

'Leave the room, Peter! I want to talk to Olive.'

'What' all the fu'? She on'y anima'.'

'Out, Peter, out!'

He struggled to his feet, lurched towards the door and said to Olive with ominous malice as he passed her: 'Look wha' yer done!'

Angela pushed him through the door and closed it.

'I'm sorry, love.'

'Angela, I'm not your love.'

'Now that isn't nice, when we've been so close.'

'Well, I'm sick of it – you took over my father, you do your best to take over my dogs, you've taken over my home, and your son tortures my poor old pet. It can't go on, it can't. When are you buying your house? Did you ever mean to? I can't live my life at this rate – you'll have to go with Peter.'

'We will tomorrow.'

'He must, Angela, you must see it. He's not civilised, he's awful.'

'You'll soon be rid of him.'

'Do you promise?'

'I'll return him to his father.'

'I don't mean you have to go.'

'Are you apologising, Olive?'

'Yes, if you like.'

'I'll accept your apology. Try to calm down, dear!'

'Don't be so dignified! I lost my temper, I can't bear cruelty.'

'I know.'

'Thanks for understanding.'

'You'll be better soon.'

'I won't. I'll be worse. This is getting worse and worse, and I'm more and more miserable.'

It was no exaggeration, Olive had realised she was miserable and feared she would be more so. Her imagination was against her, she imagined that evil forces had decided to do her down.

She was an orphan, all alone, and felt exposed and unprotected. She had her home and a nurse in attendance, and Peggy and Denis, she had no money worries, yet her nerves were strained as never before. She had never suffered from the 'poor little me' syndrome – her state of mind verging towards paranoia was a new experience. Peter's visit might account for it all, but Peter had gone, Peter was not coming back, according to Angela, and Olive was still apprehensive, more apprehensive, and wondered if she was about to be ill.

Fate, as is well-known, is not a gentleman, and likes nothing better than to kick a person when he or she is hurt, weakened, incapable of resistance.

Trix had been injured internally as well as externally by Peter's attentions. She was old, accustomed to nothing but kindness, and the shock of having a heavy rider on her back, beating her with maximum force, affected her heart. One morning Olive found her dead in the paddock – she lay on her side with all four legs stretched out stiffly, as if she had been a wooden horse.

The death, not counting its probable cause, was a minor tragedy; but Olive traced the chain of events that killed Trix, and her other four-legged friends, to her own abdication of responsibility, blamed herself, and suffered major distress. If only, if only, was the refrain of her attempt to put two and two together. She had done so many things she ought not to have done: left Trix within striking distance of Peter, failed to take Peter's hint that he had a yen to ride her, admitted Peter into The Old Hundred and her life, colluded with her father's matrimonial madness, failed to get rid of Angela when she was simply an employee.

An initiative to ease the passing of her darling mother had been allowed to transform itself into a cat's cradle of alliances, family ties, emotional obligations, moral uncertainties, and incontrovertible irreversible facts. There was a ring on Angela's finger, she was entitled to live at The Old Hundred, she was Olive's stepmother, and she had retained her dignity when Olive lost hers.

These unconstructive reflections triggered by the death of Trix spread like an infection into every corner of Olive's being. Was Angela wicked, for instance – had she laid a curse on the house of Crighton? How many more deaths were due to follow those which had so far occurred? Should the nettle be grasped now, belatedly, before there was even more stinging? Should assistance be sought, say from Martin East?

Olive shook herself at work or in the small hours, whenever she was dogged by these terrible questions. Angela was good, her good friend, she insisted, and the existence of Peter was nobody's crime. Of course she could not ask Angela to disregard the terms of her husband's will and leave The Old Hundred. Martin was a lawyer, and no law had been broken as yet – anyway, Olive remembered her father's opinion that when law comes in through the front door justice flies out of the window.

She shook herself, and clung on to her disappearing sense of proportion. She refused to believe that she was engaged in any contest. She recalled the fun she had with Angela, the jokes, and what a fine nurse she was, giving confidence and knowing how to make a patient comfortable. Peter had gone, a new era of settling for her circumstances, her lonely state, her spinster-hood, needed to be welcomed with open arms rather than shied away and shrunk from.

Nevertheless the corpse of Trix, or perhaps the ghost of Trix, seemed to create a mental obstacle between herself and Angela.

She found more work to do in order to have less time for her thoughts. Tim Spell at the Surgery told her she looked wan, and ought to take it easier, so often that she could have screamed. Her colleagues said that if they were in her position they would pack it in, be a lady of leisure, travel round the world, open her house and garden to the public – counter-productive advice. Peggy fussed over her and Denis was apt to inquire: 'You got the yellow jaundice, Miss?' Only Angela spared her refer-ences to her appearance and health.

Angela, sensing Olive's crisis and respecting her privacy, behaved with perfect tact, and Olive, contrarily, was the more irritated by her for doing so. She was grateful and annoyed sim-ultaneously, she loved and hated Angela, and wondered if she would burst under pressure from the mixed feelings building up inside her.

After one bad day at work – too much going on, too many dogs to cremate – she was in no hurry to return home. She rang through to Angela to warn that she would be late, and reacted ungratefully to the news that Angela had already taken Buddy and Whisper for their evening walk. In the Fiesta, instead of looking forward to The Old Hundred and time to relax, she felt as if her hackles were rising – she was also increasingly short of breath.

Whatever was wrong with her was alarmingly uncharacteristic, and she struggled in vain to regain her own kind of normality. She walked into the house, was greeted by her dogs, but half-heartedly after their walk, and kissed as usual by an Angela who was fully made-up and dressed unusually in a smart silk dress and high-heeled shoes.

'What's this in aid of?' she inquired.

Angela seized her hand and led her into the dining-room, not the kitchen where they ate as a rule, saying, 'Look, look!'

The candles in the candelabra in the centre of the table were lit and illuminated the otherwise dark room, wine had been decanted and the best plates and serving dishes were on the hot-plate on the sideboard – it was like the happy days when Olive was young and her mother was in charge of the house.

A huge lump in her throat almost stifled her.

Angela was saying, 'It's to celebrate for a change, it's to surprise you and cheer you up.'

Olive found her voice and demanded: 'What have I got to celebrate? What are you celebrating?'

And she began to cry bitterly, suspiciously, furiously.

She could not stop. Only by crying could she reduce the size of the blockage of her windpipe, it seemed. She cried uncontrollably. She cried for everything that had happened since her mother fell ill.

Angela patted, stroked, soothed, comforted

her, she begged and then ordered her to desist, she wrung her hands and said she had meant well and was sorry, all to no avail.

At length she went across to the sideboard, rummaged in the cupboard where a variety of bottles of alcohol were stored, mixed a potion in a glass, and, kneeling beside Olive who sat on a dining-room chair, bent forwards and retching painfully, she held Olive's head with one hand and with the other raised the glass to her lips.

'Drink this, love – it'll make you feel so much better – just a sip at a time – please, love!'

It had some of the desired effect. The violent part of Olive's crying turned into sobs and hiccups, and she accepted the offer of tissues from Angela. Gradually she sought to explain herself, but was too weak to launch into the reasons why she was sick at heart. The liquid she had swallowed was deliciously sweet and soft, and when the glass was empty Angela refilled it.

'What am I drinking?' Olive murmured.

'Nurse's Friend, that's what we used to call it. Rum's the main ingredient.'

'Won't you have some?'

'Well, I might – thank you.'

In time Olive said: 'The food you cooked will be spoilt – and you took so much trouble.'

'It's chicken livers with rice and spinach,' Angela replied, 'you like that, don't you?'

'Yes – I did – but not tonight – forgive me.'

'You ought to eat a bit after the drinks.'

'Well, a tiny bit.'

They sat at the dining-room table, Olive at

the head, Angela on her right, in the place of the guest of honour. The decanter circulated in the old style, and even the small quantity of wine Olive swallowed acted like oil on troubled water. Her hostility was superseded by general benevolence, and by her reinforced friendship with her companion.

She repaid Angela's questions about her health – was she all right, was she better? – by asking how Angela was, really and truly.

'Are you talking about my private life?'

'I am.'

'Don't worry your head on that account.'

'I want you to be happy.'

'That's nice of you, love. Same to you! But my private life's a bore right now. It's worse, it's non-existent.'

'No What's-his-name?'

'Not a squeak out of him.'

'Bad luck.'

'Oh well – he came in handy – there's no handyman in view at present.'

'Poor Angela!'

'Sex is stupid. You don't remember it when it's available, and when it isn't you can't forget it. You wouldn't understand, would you, my love?'

'Of course I would.'

'But you're still intact.'

'What do you mean?'

'Still a virgin.'

'I've learnt a lot from you.'

'Most men are more hell than heaven. But here's hoping your man's the exception.'

'Who knows?'

The evening wore on, and wine loosened the tongues of both women, Angela to indulge her pornographic fancy, Olive to ask her to shut up, not to be vulgar and crude, which had the opposite effect.

At one point Angela expatiated on the opportunities afforded by a shower. She was sexually inspired by the fall of warm water on her head and body, she explained. She regretted the absence of a shower in The Old Hundred.

Olive's attention had been wandering, but she distinctly heard the following: 'I like to be washed, you see. In a shower I'm like a flower in the sun and any old bee can sip my nectar. If you installed a shower here...'

Olive interrupted: 'I'm going to faint.'

Her head drooped forward, she could no longer hold it up, she was terrified in case she was sick, and she lost consciousness.

She came to with a thumping headache, and painfully opened her eyes in a dark strange room. She was again insensible for an unmeasured lapse of time, and woke to the realisation that she was naked. She was startled, cried out – she always slept in a nightgown – threw back the covers and sat up. Morning light stole between the curtains – she was in her mother's room, in the double bed slept in by Angela, and Angela was in it with her, waking and stretching.

Olive's first panicky question was beside almost every point: 'Where are my clothes?'

'On the chair,' Angela replied, yawning.

'Why am I here?'

'You passed out.'

'I should be in my room.'

'Beggars can't be choosers, sweetie. You weren't in a fit state to choose anything. I wasn't going to have another member of your family die on me. At least I was on the spot if you started to choke.'

'Was I ill?'

'Drunk.'

'You made me drunk.'

'There's ingratitude for you! I stopped you having hysterics and probably a fit to follow.'

'Oh heavens! What's the time?'

'Seven-thirty.'

'I'll be late for work.'

'You can't work today. Ring up and say you're ill. I'll ring Tim Spell for you. It's only the truth, Olive.'

'I'm going to dress.'

'Well, don't be shy – I undressed you last night and took you to the lavatory.'

Olive began to whimper and sob.

'Here we go again,' Angela laughed.

When Olive was more or less decent she snatched up the rest of her clothing and made for the door.

Angela called after her: 'I must say, you can be affectionate when you undo your buttons.'

Olive drew no conclusions from this sally, she scarcely took it in, yet she felt in her bones that she had made an irreparable mistake.

5

Drunkenness and a night in the wrong bed meant shame and disgrace to Olive Crighton. She was not promiscuous, feckless, easy-going, ready for anything. She was the age-old image of a chaste innocent girl who has not left home. She looked prim and discouraging to outsiders, maybe, but she saw herself, she thought of herself if or when she did think of herself, as pure in spirit. She had failed to find earthy love, maybe, but she loved passionately and with all her heart an ideal created by art, of the linkage for life of strong souls aspiring towards perfection. She had lost her metaphysical virginity – her ideal had been defaced – ugliness had staggered into the picture – she had become nearly unrecognisable in her own eyes.

She recoiled from the remembrance. It took her days to piece outward events together logically and in sequence. Time at last enabled her to see where she had gone wrong. She should not have allowed her feelings to accumulate like water behind a dam. She should not have let the dam burst for so slight a reason as it had – rationally, what was unbearable about a meal prepared for her with all the trimmings? She should not have cried so hysterically as to need the assistance of alcohol. She should then not have drunk wine, and above all she should not have entrusted her person absolutely to Angela.

Life went on – they were still living together. Angela sometimes made half-humorous references to alcoholic refreshment – 'Are you in the mood for a blockbuster, love? ... A tiny glass of wine won't knock you out for eight hours, my dear' – and Olive would have to smile at them tightly. But either carelessness or discretion on Angela's part gave Olive leave to gloss over the incident and try to behave as if nothing untoward had happened.

While she was putting herself together again as best she could, she was rung up by Martin East and invited to tea on the coming Sunday. She accepted eagerly, then attempted to rationalise her lack of hesitation and her noticeable heartbeats. Sunday was her day off and now she would not have to spend the whole of the Sunday in question with Angela. Naturally she was pleased to hear a strong sensible male voice again, and somehow sure that Martin's mother would be a kind straightforward woman. Besides, it was normal of her to feel flattered.

The Easts' home was a late Victorian or early Edwardian villa standing in its own garden in a residential road, Meridian Road, in Warminster. It was in apple pie order, and the garden was full of flowers. Martin welcomed her by shaking her hand in both of his, and escorted her into a large light drawing-room where a white-haired lady sat with a dog at her feet beside a circular white-clothed table laid for tea.

Mrs East apologised for not getting up to welcome the visitor.

'I'm chairbound, and this is my dear dog Winnie who's even older than I am and can only wag her tail at you. Winnie used to be a mongrel, but age has lent her a certain distinction – we must all hope the same thing happens to human beings. I would not talk about my dog if I hadn't been told that you're a dog-lover, and not one of those inhuman people who have no understanding of their fellow creatures and hate dogs for being better than they are. Please come and sit down. I'm so pleased to meet you, as I also happen to know that you love music, opera in particular, just as I do, and there aren't a great many of us in Wiltshire. May I call you Olive? Are you managing on your own at The Old Hundred, Olive?'

Mrs East had not turned into another of the monologuists of senior citizenry. She spoke well and amusingly, she conversed, and her gentle wit and sensitive spirit reminded Olive of her mother. Mrs East's treatment of the English language was wonderful to hear after Angela's workaday speech and, even more so, after Peter's massacre of his mother tongue. Olive's mind expanded – a sensation comparable to the inhalation of concentrated oxygen – while her enjoyment was bitterly sweet, since it was both nostalgic and cognisant that she would soon be gasping for air in the verbal pollution of her home.

They moved on from dogs to music. Martin went to boil a kettle and fetch the sandwiches and cake, and his mother confessed to a preference for the more romantic composers, for the Verdi of *Traviata* and the Richard Strauss of *Rosenkavalier*, whereas Olive said that recently she had developed a love of Monteverdi and Mozart's *Don Giovanni*.

'Not many operas are happy,' Mrs East observed. 'They don't have happy endings as a rule.'

'I'm afraid they're like life,' Olive suggested.

'Yes, but they make life and death beautiful for us – they comfort and inspire us by presenting our joys and sorrows more beautifully than they often are in reality.'

Martin wove another matching strand into the sociability. He spared Olive any reference to the situation at The Old Hundred, and instead asked about her work with Tim Spell and slipped pieces of interesting information into the natural flow of the conversation. It was a lovely occasion – the light room without net curtains, the pretty interior decoration, the overwhelmingly friendly host and hostess, and the exchange of ideas.

Olive stole a glance at her watch and was worried to see how late it was.

Mrs East replied to her goodbye thus: 'I can't ask you to come again, I'm too old and you're too young for that, but do remember how delighted I would be if you ever felt like coming to see me. It's been a great pleasure to meet you, and now I shall think of you whenever I listen to an opera.'

Martin followed her out of doors to the Fiesta.
'May I ring you again, Olive?' he inquired.

'Well, I hope you'll come to The Old Hundred. Yes – yes, of course. Goodbye.'

She drove away, smiling and waving. But in the car memories of that ghastly night pounced upon her. Angela's parting shot on the morning after, that she could be or had been affectionate when her buttons were undone, what did it mean? She had never heard the phrase about the undoing of buttons – but she felt herself undone. Had she participated in some horrendous rite between women? Her face flushed scarlet – she knew how scarlet it·must be because it burned, and she was soon sweating profusely. She was terrified of Martin ever getting to know she had slept with Angela. She was mortified to think of Martin's mother discovering she had been dead drunk and possibly involved in lesbian practices. She was not sure that she could face up to the future. And for some minutes in her car was almost sure that she could not.

But she drove down a country lane, stopped the car, breathed deeply, prayed for strength, and when her heart had ceased to thump she returned to The Old Hundred.

Angela's interest in her visit was slight and reassuring.

'Did you have fun?'

'Yes, thanks.'

'Nice people?'

'Yes, very.'

'I hope Martin's attitude was more private than professional.'

'What do you mean?'

'Did he kiss you?'

'No!'

'What a swizz!'

At least Angela was promoting heterosexuality without reservations.

And music, as always, came to Olive's rescue. She had moved her musical apparatus upstairs, and now listened to her recordings in her own bedroom, where she was definitely not to be disturbed. Privacy was another healing treatment, and not for the first time she thanked heaven that the attempt to educate Angela musically had fallen flat.

About a fortnight passed. Olive and Angela did not clash, yet the telltale effect on Olive of their relations was that she suffered from a stiff neck caused by tension.

Then one evening after supper Angela announced casually: 'My little boy's in hot water again.'

She was smoking a cigarette and sipping a cup of black coffee, and her bright blue eyes behind her fringe looked watchful to Olive.

'Oh?'

'It's his blasted father.'

'What's happened?'

'He's going to be homeless.'

'I can't have Peter here, Angela.'

'Nor can I. He's as much a menace to me as

he was to you. I'm so sorry you were saddled with him. This time round I've told him to get a job and find himself a lodging.'

'What did he say to that?'

'Not a lot.'

'What can he do? What's he willing to do?'

'He's strong. He could find work as a labourer or on a building site. I refuse to take sole responsibility for him. His father must do his bit – he got all the joy out of making Peter, my share was more pain than I expected.'

'You do agree, don't you, that The Old Hundred isn't the right place for him, even short-term?'

'Sure! I'm on your side. The question is, will he agree with you and me?'

'Have you told him he's not wanted?'

'I've tried. But you know how hard it is to get any sense into his head. He's seventeen and a half, and a free agent, I'm sorry to say.'

'You mean he might turn up on the doorstep?'

'I can't rule it out.'

'But, Angela, he'd ruin everything, my home, my life.'

'And mine, frankly.'

'What are we to do?'

'I don't know. I suppose we'll have to do the usual feminine thing, wait and see. I'm going to have another shot at his father, and I promise to keep you in the picture.'

'Thanks,' Olive concluded wryly.

A day or two later she left a note for Angela before she motored to work.

It ran: 'Dear A, I've been thinking, and the fact is I can't allow Peter to stay in my house. Last time, it was a disaster. Sorry – once bitten etc! Love.'

She regretted it, of course – hot letters are always more regrettable than hot words. In the evening, when she dared to return, Angela behaved exactly as usual, had cooked the supper and chatted exclusively about humdrum matters.

The end of it was that Olive had to ask, to blurt out in a breathless rush, the query as to whether or not her note had been received.

'Sure! Poor love, having to write to me formally – my family must have burrowed under your skin – what a shame!'

'Are there any developments, Angela?'

'I'm sorrier than ever to say there are. Peter's father's been as much use as a sick headache. All the help he's given me is the time that Peter's train arrives in Bath.'

'When is he arriving?'

'Tomorrow afternoon.'

'You didn't tell me that, you said you'd keep me in the picture.'

'I didn't know until earlier today, sweetie.'

'He can't.'

'I know, I know – but that's wishful thinking.'

'Oh Angela!'

'Don't be angry with me, dear. I'm upset too – and it won't do any good for us to start screaming at each other.'

'How long is he coming for?'

'You know I can't answer that question.'

88

'But he's nothing to do with me.'

'I'll let you have Peter's father's telephone number if you like – perhaps he won't dare to curse you.'

'No, no – I'll talk to Martin East.'

'Men don't care for women who beg for favours and expect them to work miracles.'

'It's not only personal. At the Surgery they mentioned something called an injunction.'

'Olive, my dear, I wouldn't go down the legal road.'

'Why not? I won't be bullied and have advantage taken of me – I won't, Angela! It's been happening for too long.'

'I haven't taken advantage of any member of your family. Your father married me in spite of my advice and against my will.'

'Really? Well, if we're going back to my father, he left me this house – I own it – and I'll have the locks on the doors changed if necessary, I'll go to court if I have to, in order not to admit any lout who thinks he can move into my home when he pleases.'

'Olive, you're forgetting the right your father bequeathed to me.'

'I'm not – that was for you – not for you and Peter – my father would turn in his grave if Peter broke into The Old Hundred.'

'Peter's my flesh and blood. Think carefully, sweetie. It wouldn't look good in a court for you to stop my son seeing his mother, and vice versa. How many empty bedrooms have you got? You wouldn't wish to be branded as mean and selfish. No, wait, there's another point that's worth a second thought. I'd have to tell the truth, the whole truth, in court. Do you see what I'm driving at?'

'No, I do not!'

'If I was asked, I'd have to describe our relationship.'

'What are you hinting at, Angela?'

'Our cuddle in bed.'

'I never cuddled you. I was unconscious – you made the story up to blackmail me.'

'Very well, Olive, here's the bottom line! You deny our cuddle – but it's your word against mine, isn't it? And your reputation would be on the floor by the time I'd finished with you. Mud sticks, remember! And don't you forget Martin – he'd think more than twice about marrying a woman with mud all over her.'

She cried. She was defeated again. In the end she was consoled, embraced, urged not to worry, picked up and dusted down, by the victor.

The injustice grated on her soul. She thought she was Angela's superior, not merely in a snobbish sense, although, undeniably, she was better-bred. Class factors apart, she was more cultured, more appreciative of the finer products and aspects of civilisation, even in an academic sense more intelligent. Yet she was apparently no match for her sly and unscrupulous inferior.

How hard it is for idealists to discover that might is right!

Angela had the grace to try to soften her hard line. She had a corner to fight for, she explained, and pleaded for forgiveness.

'I couldn't let you discard me and banish me without a little bit of a struggle. I'm so fond of you, and was so fond of your father, that I was in a panic in case, because of Peter, you'd overlook all we've been to each other and all I've done for you. I don't mean to brag, but I have given a good deal to the Crighton family, haven't I, sweetie? I'm not going to drag you into court – it's unthinkable – but occasionally we have to be realistic and find out where we really stand. As a matter of fact, I couldn't afford to go to law about anything, and I wouldn't dare. I'm sorry to have such a troublesome son, but you do see that I'm the one being blackmailed and bullied in the first place, don't you? There, there, love, don't take our disagreement so much to heart! Listen, we've lived together for months with scarcely a shadow between us, and that's most unusual, we haven't behaved like cats or female dogs, we have reason to be rather proud. And between you and me and these four walls, I've never fancied my own sex, that's the truth. I will admit you're a prettier person to undress than many I've seen in the buff, you're a holiday to look at, but looking's not doing, is it? Dry your eyes, here's my tissue.'

The unintended consequences of this speech were that it fanned the flames and failed to allay the fears in Olive's innermost being.

The next morning, while she was preparing to

go to work, Angela came downstairs in her dressing-gown and urged a truce for later in the day and in future.

'I'll give Peter the strongest talking-to he's ever had, and if you could let him have his head and the benefit of the doubt we might get along together okay,' she said.

'You know my feelings,' Olive replied.

'They're the problem,' Angela laughed.

'I'll be polite.'

'And not too frosty, love?'

'No,' Olive equivocated.

She returned later than usual that evening. The house was ablaze with light and pop music blared through the open front door. She slammed out of the Fiesta and strode in.

Angela with Peter in tow met her in the hall. He had shaved his head but not his bristly beard.

He called in a loud voice, 'Hi, Olive,' stepped forward more quickly than she expected, enfolded her in a bear-hug and tried to kiss her on the lips, not sexually but in line with the convention of his class.

She pushed him away, but he clearly did not consider he had been repulsed.

'Ta for havin' me, Olly. Thi' ol' place i' my secon' 'ome, Olly. A goo' boy fro' now on, tha's wha' I'm goin' to be, see? You ha' no fear, Olly, Pete's 'ere, no sweat!'

She asked him to turn down the volume of the telly, returned the greeting of her dogs, who were also showing signs of stress, went into the

92

kitchen, where a meal had been prepared by Angela.

'We hoped you'd eat with us,' Angela said.

'I can't,' Olive replied. 'I'm sorry. Peter, I'm sorry. I've had a long day, and all I want is a tray in my room and to go to sleep. I hope you'll understand. I'll put the dogs out later, and I'll be very grateful if you keep the noise down. Will you lock up, Angela? Thanks. I'll just help myself and disappear.'

'Ni'-ni', Olly, min' the fleas don' bi',' Peter sniggered.

It was a similar story. It was a sadder story, because Peter already knew the house and how to clog up its workings. He was idle and destructive simultaneously, an oppressive presence, with a twisted sense of humour and a malicious streak. He was clever enough to have bad ideas, that only 'bloo'y foo's' worked if they could get money for not working, and that toffs were fair game for the 'Robi' Hoo's' of the criminal fraternity. He was dirty in his habits, untidy, quarrelsome with his mother and fresh with Olive.

He was responsible for Peggy's resignation and departure: 'I can't keep him at bay, Miss Olive.' She walked out one day, explaining apologetically that she could not bear to argue with or say goodbye to the Malones. She was years past retiring age – Olive did not like to press her to stay on, and understood exactly why she was in a hurry to leave. They parted with tears and promises to keep in touch as neighbours.

Angela undertook all the cooking, lunch as well as dinner, and to do the housework. She complicated this issue, too – she rejected Olive's offer to employ someone else to render menial services not suited to Lady Crighton, and then refused to accept payment for rendering them herself.

Olive no longer left Buddy and Whisper at The Old Hundred in the daytime. They accompanied her to work and were placed in the safe keeping of Helen Spell, Tim's wife. She ate bread and cheese and an apple at midday, and fed her dogs either out of doors or in the Fiesta.

She was no longer what she had been before Peter re-entered her life. She had become an escapist, she escaped him by imprisoning herself, sneaking in and out of her own house and locking herself in her bedroom.

The next hazard on Olive's *via dolorosa* was heralded by the unholy din of Peter's motorbike, bought for him by his mother. It was second-hand, powerful, noisy, and sinister to boot – was Peter settling in for a long stay? Angela's attitude was predicable – it would keep him out of everybody's way, carry him to and from the job he intended to get, and so on. Olive confined her response with difficulty to insisting he was not to ride the bike anywhere on her premises except in one of the paddocks and up and down the drive.

One rainy evening she was approached by Denis as she stepped out of her car. It was six-thirty, long after the five o'clock finish of his day's work, and he was clearly agitated and nearly crying.

He answered her questions by leading her round the side of the house and pointing out the lawn, cut up by tyre-marks of Peter's motor-bike and mostly mud.

Olive consoled him or tried to, went indoors, reached her father's study, shut and locked the door, and punched in the telephone number of Martin's home.

She had been pining to do so for days. She needed a man to turn to in her predicament, one particular man. She had been determined to take nothing for granted. She had been inhibited by Angela's hold over her good name. But anger and necessity overruled all her scruples.

Martin answered.

'Oh Martin!'

Instantly she was soothed, she was overcome by shyness and excitement.

'Is that Olive?'

'Yes.'

'How are you?'

'Sorry to bother you.'

'I'm glad you have bothered.'

'Could you have tea here one day? There's something I'd like you to see for yourself.'

'I'd love to.'

'Could you have tea on Sunday next, the day after tomorrow?'

He replied that he thought so.

'It's quite important, it's quite urgent actually.'

'Is anything wrong, Olive?'

'Yes and no. Please come!'

'Of course I will.'

Later, when she felt she would lose neither her temper nor her head, she spoke to the two Malones as they were settling down to their supper and she was carrying her tray of food to eat upstairs.

'Oh Peter,' she said, 'you've ridden your motorbike on my lawn and wrecked it.'

'I've told him, sweetie,' Angela interposed.

'Solly, Olly,' he sniggered – it was one of his jokes to rhyme 'sorry' with his impudent version of her Christian name.

'You're not to do that ever again, Peter.'

'Go' the messa' lou' and clear, Olly.'

'Angela,' Olive continued, 'Martin East's coming to tea next Sunday and he'd like to see you again. Shall we all have tea together?'

'Yes, love – that sounds nice – but I can't guarantee Peter's attendance – he's so mad on his bike.'

'Will you have tea with us on Sunday, Peter?' Olive inquired.

'I don' min'.'

'No, Peter – do you promise to have tea on Sunday?'

'Cro' my hear' – anythi' for you, Olly.'

'Thanks.'

Sunday arrived eventually. Angela baked a cake and Olive cut sandwiches, and tea was laid in the dining-room. She ran out to greet Martin on the gravel sweep.

'What is it, Olive? I've been concerned,' he began.

'Thank you so much. Thank you for answering my SOS.'

'Well, I was hoping to see you anyway. I would have rung you if you hadn't rung me. I'm glad to be here.'

'Come in,' she said.

Setting aside small talk, the relevant exchanges at the dining-room table were as follows.

Martin asked Angela: 'How are you getting on with your house-hunting?'

Angela replied: 'Not much progress – everything's awfully expensive round here.'

'I hear of houses for sale in the course of my work. If an interesting one turned up, I could let you have details.'

'That's good of you. Shall I pass your teacup along to Olive?'

Peter weighed in: 'Wha's tha', Angie? You buyin' 'ouses or wha'?'

'It's nothing, Peter.'

'A 'ouse ain't nothin', Ange. You bee' tellin' me porkies. You go' a 'ouse and you're keepin' it for yoursel'.'

'I haven't got any house. We'll sort this out later.'

'No ti' like presen'. Tha's the tru', i'n't it, Marti'? Spi' the bea's, Angie – where do you ge' the loll'?'

'Shut up, Peter!'

'I'll ge' i' ou' of you, no sweat – you know tha', Ange, I'll squee' you ti' you squea'.'

At this point Martin changed the subject.

'What do you do, Peter?'

'Nothin'! Ask a stupi' question, Marti'. I'm a gen'lema' of leis' ri' now. Go' the plo', Marti'?'

The tea party was over. Olive walked Martin to his car.

'How long has this been going on?' he asked her.

'Too long – this is Peter's second visit – and he's the last straw.'

'Is Angela all the other straws?'

'Yes – but it's such a complicated story – I don't know if I could ever tell it.'

'I must study your father's will and have a think. Are you safe? Do you feel safe?'

'I don't know, I suppose so.'

'That moron's unacceptable – I hate to think of you having to put up with him.'

'He's what I wanted you to see.'

'Can you manage here for the time being?'

'Just about.'

'You know you can ring me any time, and I'd love you to do that. Let me know at once if there's any criminal activity.'

'Thank you, Martin.'

'Your welfare means an awful lot to me. Can I ring you soon?'

'Not at The Old Hundred, ring me at Tim Spell's Surgery.'

'I will.'

Angela on that same day, when she was alone with Olive, commented on Peter's behaviour.

'I'm afraid he didn't do well. I'm damn sure he embarrassed me. But he won't be corrected, he's deaf to anything he doesn't want to hear. I can't cope with him at all – that's the whole story, love.'

'Can't he go back to his father?'

'Not a chance – his father says he'll call in the police if he sets eyes on Peter again. Anyhow, Peter refuses to leave me.'

'Why don't you buy a house? Seriously, why don't you, Angela?'

'In my walk of life, questions like that aren't asked. You couldn't imagine what's become of my legacy, could you?'

'Have you spent it?'

'The best part's paid my debts.'

'Such big debts?'

'Overdraft at bank and on credit cards – you'd be surprised, dear, how the rest of us live.'

'Sorry – I am sorry – but, really, it's not my business, Angela.'

'True enough! Why should you worry on that account? We're giving you enough headaches, aren't we? Look, I'll have another shot at Peter. I'll try to get him to help Denis straighten up the lawn.'

'For goodness sake don't do that – tell him to leave Denis strictly alone.'

'Very well. But he should make amends to you or somebody.'

'Forget it, Angela. Think of a way of getting Peter out of The Old Hundred!'

'You know I'll do my best, love.'

A few days later Martin rang Olive at work

99

and asked her out to lunch. She agreed to meet him at the pub in the picturesque village of Stonefield.

The spring weather was fine, sunny, balmy. They greeted each other without physical contact, and helped themselves to food and sat at a bench-table out of doors. Buddy and Whisper were with them, and were much admired by Martin.

He talked business without delay.

'I've pondered your father's will, and asked a colleague for his advice. We both believe that only Angela has a legal right to stay at The Old Hundred, and in a court of law we don't think she would be granted permission to stay there open-endedly together with her adult son.'

'I couldn't sue her in court, Martin.'

'No – she's your stepmother – I understand and respect your kind heart – but you can't live with that moronic hooligan – and I dread to think of the difficulties you must have had with his mother.'

'I feel bound by my father's wishes.'

'Then we'd better try to get her to find alternative accommodation.'

'She's run through my father's bequest.'

'How's she done that?'

'She says it's paid her debts.'

'Well, I believe every adult in our poor old country is meant to carry thousands of pounds of debt. But surely no bank or credit company would let her accumulate such a lot of debt without taking punitive action. Is she truthful?'

'I don't think so.'

'Who paid for the son's motorbike?'

'She did.'

'She's a State Registered Nurse, she could earn well and easily obtain a mortgage. Has anyone mentioned a mortgage? Almost everybody buys property by borrowing against its value.'

'I didn't know that – I'm so ignorant – Angela holds it against me.'

'You know things she's never dreamt of.'

'How do you know?'

He laughed and said: 'Shall I write and give her some figures – her possible salary, the sort of mortgage she could obtain? I might look out a house or two that would be within her range of options.'

'What bearing would your letter have on my life?'

'Are you afraid of the Malones?'

'No, but ... I don't want our cohabitation to become even more tricky.'

'I'll be diplomatic and write in a friendly way, a note in my own handwriting. There's almost bound to be a crunch somewhere along the line – it seems unavoidable. I can't let you house Peter and his mother for the rest of your life or theirs.'

'No.'

'I'll back you to the hilt whatever happens. You won't be alone in seeking to repossess your home.'

'Thank you very much.'

The subject was apparently exhausted. It was

too nice, sitting there in the sun, beside a tinkling streamlet, near willow trees and with views of the wide village street, to dwell upon nastiness. They ate and smiled at each other, eyes half-closed against the brightness.

'How's your mother?'

'Fine! She sent you her love.'

'Give her mine.'

He thought for a moment and informed her: 'I love my mother, but I'm not a mother's boy, if you know what I mean. I stay at home because it's convenient for all concerned, and because, until a year ago, I had an emotional commitment elsewhere.'

'Oh?'

'I'm not committed any more. Are you, Olive? Pardon the direct question.'

'No,' she murmured, 'no' – conveying a fraction of her meaning.

'May I think of you as one day becoming more than a friend of mine?'

'Oh Martin!'

'No need to answer now – don't answer quickly, please – take your time.'

'It's not that.'

'I realise you hardly know me. But I feel I know you so well.'

'You can't know everything – I don't want to give you a false impression.'

'Shall I shut up?'

'No! No, but please, just at present...'

'Point taken – I understand – you mustn't worry.'

'Oh thank you, Martin.'

A pause ensued. Much to Olive's surprise she was not embarrassed by these exchanges, nor by the silence that now fell between them. Stranger still, she was not anxious that she had, could or would let him slip through her fingers.

Martin said: 'This is where a lot of the stone used to build Bath was quarried. You see the dressed stones in the walls of those cottages – they were the rejects, the stones that split or cracked, which cottage builders bought cheap.'

She indicated interest, but mentioned regretfully that she ought to be getting back to work.

'So must I.'

She dared to say: 'Martin, I've enjoyed it more than I can tell you.'

'Same here,' he replied.

They stood up. She shepherded her dogs to the Fiesta, and in turn was shepherded in a way that gave her a new pleasure and satisfaction.

He kissed her on the cheek goodbye. She drove off, and a mile down the road stopped and waited for her heart to beat more normally.

She could not help feeling happy as never before until early the next morning, before she left The Old Hundred, when she saw an envelope addressed to Angela from Tyndall and East.

6

Olive was nervous all day. Her dread was that Angela would twist Martin's advice so that it served her own interests rather than those of the person he intended to benefit. She anticipated another defeat.

She reached The Old Hundred at seven o'clock. Angela was standing by her car and Peter was piling suitcases into the luggage compartment. Olive immediately assumed it was too good to be true.

'What's happening?' she asked.

'Oh, Olive, I've been waiting for you. I wanted to say goodbye.'

'Why? Where are you going?'

'I've landed another engagement. I'm going to look after an old lady.'

'Is Peter going with you?'

'No. He can't. He'll be staying here in the meanwhile.'

Peter now put his oar in: 'You an' me together, Olly, we'll be havin' a high ol' ti.'

Olive said to Angela: 'Please come indoors for a moment – I must speak to you.'

They spoke in the study.

'Why are you doing this?' Olive began.

'Simple, sweetie – your friend Martin's muscled in on the act, he's written to encourage me to earn my living, and I'm doing as I'm told.'

'I'm sure he meant nothing like that.'

'How are you sure, Olive? Did you put him up to it?'

Olive bit her tongue.

'No, he only wanted to help you, I know he wanted to help.'

'He says I should work hard in order to get a mortgage and buy a house, and incidentally rid you of my presence.'

'Oh Angela, you're taking it in the wrong way. You can't leave me alone with Peter.'

'Oh but I can. You're obliged to support my effort to find somewhere else to live.'

'How long are you going for?'

'It depends.'

'How can I contact you?'

'Peter has telephone numbers.'

'I wish you'd stay here.'

'It's a little late to say so, dear,' Angela wound up.

Olive called after her: 'Who's feeding Peter?'

'He'll eat at the pub midday, and do for himself in the evenings,' Angela called over her shoulder.

Trouble bred troubles for Olive without delay. Peter caught her in the kitchen on that first evening of their cohabitation, and accused her of unfriendliness. She had to argue that she was just tired, she had nothing against him, was neither a snob nor a bitter old maid, before she could escape with her supper of sardines, toast, apple and banana. But then she heard him banging about in the kitchen, preparing his 'fry-up', and was afraid he would set the house on fire. Later she worried about the locks on the front and side doors: she knew he could not be depended upon to turn the keys and slide all the bolts, yet was afraid to lock herself in with him.

In the morning she found the kitchen in a filthy state and had to clean it. In the evening Peter informed her that he was biking back to the pub for better 'nosh an' comp'ny' than was on offer at The Old Hundred. As a result, she lay awake until she heard the roar of his motor-bike and his stumbling and belching entry into the house, a safe time after which she stole downstairs to see to the locks.

She could not entirely avoid him. He would join her for breakfast in his pyjamas, or corner her while she prepared her supper. And his conversation became increasingly lewd.

'No crumpet in Luffie', Olly. Wha's a man to do? Wha' do girlies do if they ain' ge'ing it from a man? Are you goin' to tell me, Olly? No, you'd li' me to tell you, wou'nt you, Olly?'

One evening he banged on her bedroom door and told her to 'stuff tha' racke'' – a recording of Strauss's *Four Last Songs*; and later, around midnight, on another evening, he tricked her out of her bedroom by telling her he could not turn off a gas burner in the kitchen, and then propositioned her in disgusting terms.

She suffered Peter for a week without deciding to take firm action against him. The action she had in mind was to speak to Martin East; but she had hoped to hear from Martin and been disappointed. She had expected him at least to want to know the effects of his letter, but had heard nothing. She was afraid she might have put him off, reluctant to seem to be pursuing him, and completely averse to criticising or blaming him for the impossible position in which she found herself. Result, no action was taken.

On the eighth evening at ten-thirty or eleven Peter returned from the pub and raucous voices, more than one voice, were audible. He must have brought boys back with him, they all sounded drunk, and she was sure they would do damage or pinch things, alcohol in particular. She lost her temper, put on her day clothes, went downstairs and told them – the two offending oiks – to get out of her house.

They obeyed her. Luckily they obeyed. And Peter was contrite in a maudlin manner.

'Solly, Olly,' he repeated.

She attended to locks and headed for the stairs. But he approached her and asked if he could show her something in the study. She followed him in, and he turned round and exhibited himself with his trousers undone.

He was laughing, she tried to escape, but he laid hands on her, detained her, rubbed himself against her, saying hoarsely: 'Be a spor', Olly – let's have you – don' be mean, Olly – gi' it a ki', Olly!'

She somehow freed herself. In the morning, with Denis in tow, she burst into Peter's bedroom and persuaded him to hand over a scrap of paper bearing a telephone number. She rang it and spoke to a Mrs Harris – but she was too agitated to draw any conclusion from the name. Soon Angela was on the line.

'You'll have to come back,' Olive began.

'What's happened?'

'Your son assaulted me last night.'

'Did he hurt you?'

Angela's cool scepticism exasperated Olive.

'He made a pass at me, he would have raped me – I can't stand it – please come back immediately!'

'I thought you wanted me out of your house.'

'Oh Angela, don't argue!'

'You won't set your Martin on me again?'

'No! No – Martin was only trying to help you as well as me. All I want is not to be alone with Peter. Don't make me call the police!'

'Calm down, sweetie! Shouldn't you be going to work?'

'Of course I should, but I don't want to go and return to be raped and murdered.'

'Now you are exaggerating, love.'

'Please, Angela! I'm desperate. And Martin's deserted me. I don't know what to do next. Have you started working for your old lady?'

'No. She died. All right, I'll be back. But remember, you begged me.'

* * *

Five minutes after Olive had spoken to Angela on the telephone, the postman delivered a letter to The Old Hundred, a letter from Martin, which Olive read breathlessly in the stationary Fiesta parked on the lonely road that led to her place of work.

It was from Meridian Road, dated back to the day they had lunched together at Stonefield, but must have been mislaid somehow – the post-marked date was illegible.

'Dear Olive,' it ran, 'This afternoon in the office I wrote to Angela Malone, giving her facts and figures that might encourage her to remove herself and her son from your home.

'I shall be very interested in her response, but worst luck I have been summoned down to the depths of Cornwall to sort out the estate of a deceased client. This means I shall be incom-municado for a week or ten days, but will ring you as soon as I can and hope to arrange another meeting.

'Stonefield has always pleased me, but today it had a special magic. You're faced with horrible problems, and I'd dearly love to help you to solve them. Meanwhile, and all the same, you seem to exist in a different dimension from all the cheap people. I expect you will deny it in your modest way, but in my opinion and experi-ence you spread around you a superior kind of peace, which does wonders for my spirits.

'Until we talk and are together again, Martin.'

He had not deserted her. On the contrary, he had written her a love letter in discreet terms.

But the happiness, the relief, of feeling she was not altogether alone, and might have a future beyond all expectations, was overshadowed by her realisation that soon, not some day, she would have to tackle the task of probably shattering Martin's illusions.

Angela would be sure to want to spoil her relationship with Martin, her dear ally, her protector. How would she do it? – By trying to prove, by revealing or threatening to reveal, that Olive was a pervert. She could only be stripped of her power if that episode was no longer a secret. Whatever the cost, for Martin's own sake, before he grew too serious, and to regain her own freedom, Olive must make a full confession.

Would Martin believe she was innocent? Would he still think her superior and peaceful? How could he, how could his mother, respect, let alone favour, a girl so tarnished? Had she been wrong to stifle her impulse to encourage him and hold out her open arms?

The answer to these questions was the one word, wretchedness.

Angela was the architect of her plight. But Olive in fairness had to acknowledge that without Angela she might not have been even as close to Martin as she was. She would not have been his damsel in distress, nor would she have seen him as the chivalrous knight riding to her rescue. It was through Angela's eyes that she had first realised he was desirable.

At six-thirty she was both relieved and pleased

to see the Civic on the gravel sweep. Angela came to the front door, enfolded Olive in her arms and kissed her on both cheeks. She smiled frankly, without a trace of either triumph or resentment, and said how nice it was to be back. She was a solid presence, elegantly so, and pretty too with her thatch of blond hair and the fringe shading her bright eyes.

Later they sat together in the kitchen, where one of Angela's delicious suppers was in course of preparation.

'I've given him socks,' she said.

'Where is he?'

'Upstairs, hiding, he's shy of meeting you again.'

'Shy? That's a change.'

'He's sorry, Olive.'

'He's a great one for being sorry. He scared me.'

'I know. He's going to apply for a job on that building site over Bathampton way. We must get him out of the house.'

'I'm still taking my supper upstairs.'

'Well, I understand you. Perhaps that's for the best. How are you otherwise, sweetie?'

'All right. How are you?'

'Oh, flourishing, as usual.'

'Did you look after the old lady?'

'No, she snuffed it before I could get to her.'

'I'm afraid you'll lose money by coming home to guard me.'

'Don't fret now – I'll make some money when Peter's settled – until then he's my bit of trouble, not yours.'

'Thanks, Angela. Incidentally, when I rang you, when I used the number you'd given Peter, I spoke to a Mrs Harris. Is she the wife of the solicitor who drew up Daddy's will – you told me they ran a lodging house?'

'That's right. They're the same Harrises.'

'But you said you didn't know them.'

'Did I?'

'You said you'd never heard of them until Daddy used Harris and Hurst.'

'True, but of course I got to know them afterwards.'

'I see.'

'Don't you believe me, love?'

'Yes, I do – I don't mean to hint at anything else.'

'Well, that's fine.'

Olive did not care that Angela had fibbed again.

The next day Martin East rang her at work. It was not convenient, she was busy, and would have to talk to him in the waiting room, where clients brought their dogs, cats, hamsters, pet birds. She nonetheless rushed to the telephone used by the receptionists.

'Is it a bad time?' he asked.

'No.'

'Are you well?'

'Yes, thanks.'

'What are the noises off?'

'Animals – but I can hear you.'

'Can we meet?'

'I'd love to.'

'Stonefield for lunch today or any day?'

'No, not Stonefield – I'll explain another time.'

'There's a nightclubby place, but they say it's nice for dinner.'

'Okay.'

'Will you dine with me there?'

'Please.'

'Tomorrow?'

'Yes.'

'I'll come and fetch you.'

'Don't – I could meet you.'

'No, I'd like to. Seven-thirty tomorrow at The Old Hundred?'

'Yes, Martin.'

'Goodbye.'

Anna, the receptionist on duty, inquired in a saucy undertone: 'Boyfriend?'

Olive was pleased to laugh without answering.

The day passed, and the night, and most of the following day.

Olive suffered from stress in Martin's car, and Martin, sensing her discomfort, attributed it to the advertising placards and coloured bulbs of a shed-like building bearing the name *Diner Dances*.

'Oh dear, it's a pub, it looks frightful, much worse than I guessed it might be,' he said. 'I'm sorry. Would you like to try to find somewhere else?'

'No, it's lovely,' she said.

Indoors it was better, full but not crowded, and the background muzak was inoffensive. Their table was lit by a lamp with a red shade, and they sat at a right angle to each other – Olive was relieved that they would not be face to face.

Martin ordered things to eat and drink, she wanted nothing different, and the waiter removed the menus.

'I've looked forward to seeing you,' he began.

She hesitated, she longed to reciprocate, but instead she managed to pour out in a rush: 'Martin, I've something to tell you, and it's so difficult, so difficult...'

She bit back tears and said: 'Let me go on, please! Listen, please! About a month ago I had an awful row with Angela Malone – she'd been encroaching, she never stops encroaching – and I completely lost my temper. I lost it as I never have before, because I'm not an angry type, honestly! I raged at her and then, when she gave as good as she got, when she slapped me down – verbally, I mean – I cried, I couldn't stop, I became hysterical, I suppose – it was all terrible! Angela got me a drink, she mixed me one – I don't know what was in it – rum, I believe, and other strong stuff – and she mixed me another and I drank wine as well. After that I passed out, I remember nothing that happened, and only came to the next morning.'

'That's a footnote in the biographies of most of us.'

'No, Martin, listen! I came to in my mother's

bed. Oh dear! Angela slept there when my father was alive, and she moved my father in with her when he was dying – it was their marriage bed – and she stayed put after he died. I awoke in it, in it with Angela, and without my clothes on. She had undressed me and put me to bed in case I was ill in the night, she said.'

'Don't upset yourself too much, Olive.'

'The point is, the point I have to make is that Angela suggested we had done things I can't... She was angry and said I had been affectionate while I was unconscious.'

'Rubbish!'

'Another time she said that if she needed to she would accuse me and give details publicly. She said it would be just her word against mine, but my reputation would be ruined because mud sticks. She was blackmailing me – she would blackmail me – me and you, too – so I've had to tell you – I couldn't let you think I'd deceived you. I'm sorry not to be what you thought I was, so sorry, so sorry, Martin!'

'Have my hankie.'

'Thank you.'

'Don't be sorry or sad.'

'You see, you see, I've never been like that, the thought never crossed my mind – even at school, my girls' school, I never had crushes of that kind – and now I can't read modern books where everything's topsy-turvy.'

'I believe you. Dry your eyes! What you've said does make a difference to me, it reinforces my opinion that you're honest and straight and brave.'

115

'You're very kind.'

'Not only kind – I don't exaggerate. My opinion of you goes up and my opinion of Angela takes a further dive. Do you think we could forget Angela and dwell on a less repellent subject? Here's our food.'

They smiled at each other, sipped their soup, and in time ate their next course, as they reviewed the situation at The Old Hundred.

Martin explained: 'Everyone I've asked agrees that it could be more difficult to chuck Angela out than I was hoping. She seems to be a fixture unless she chooses to go, and in that case you'd be entitled to change all the locks.'

Olive had another confession to make in the context.

'Angela left me alone with Peter ten days ago. She went to do a nursing job. He got drunk and would have raped me if I hadn't escaped – he was so frightening that I asked Angela back.'

'Oh dear!'

'Did I do wrong?'

'She could say she was at The Old Hundred to oblige you.'

'I hadn't received your letter – it arrived days late – I was unwilling to bother you, I thought you might not want to be bothered.'

'Bothered is exactly what I want to be, please remember. But how could Angela come back in the middle of nursing someone? And why did she leave – she was taking a big risk?'

116

'She was protesting against the letter you wrote her. She said you'd told her to earn money in order to buy her house.'

'I told her nothing of the sort.'

'Of course not. Anyway, the old lady she was engaged to look after died, or so she said. She was doing nothing, just lodging with Mrs Harris in Bath, the wife of Harris the solicitor. Perhaps she left Peter behind to make sure the locks were not changed.'

'No doubt. I bet she was in with Harris and Hurst all along, and it was why your father used that firm instead of mine. And I bet she was waiting for your call, to be recalled, because Harris had warned her that she would weaken her residential claim by staying away. I wouldn't be surprised if she instructed Peter to give you a fright, so that you'd invite her back. Does she know you're keeping me informed of developments?'

'You're the only person she seems to be afraid of.'

'Good. If Angela and a solicitor are putting their heads together, they must be preparing for a court case, and we'd better follow suit.'

'What shall I do, Martin?'

'Can you stick it out at home a little longer?'

'I think so. Peter won't be too bad if his mother's about.'

'He'd better be. But what a hell of a woman your stepmother is!'

Olive managed to laugh a little, and they began to talk of dogs, Cornwall, her mother and his, and their upbringings. When they had finished their dinner and were drinking coffee, a couple sitting nearby stood up and began to dance in a tiny expanse of uncarpeted flooring. They were of a certain age, and danced in a style of their own, neither the old-fashioned embrace nor modern individualistic gyrations.

Martin and Olive watched them, then Martin said: 'Shall we?'

'I'm not a good dancer,' she replied.

'You couldn't help being better than me.'

After a pause he inquired: 'Would you like to?'

Because she longed to be closer to him, as he had indicated he longed to be close to her, she said in spite of her minor uncertainties, 'Yes'.

They clasped hands and swayed to and fro to start with. But then he gently pulled her towards him, and, if distantly, they were holding each other. At last he was within range and Olive leant her forehead on his shoulder.

While they danced like that, she with her forehead on his shoulder and his arms around her, she felt she was receiving compensation for all the horrors of the recent past.

7

The next day recalled her to reality.

Before she went to work, Angela said: 'You look as if you had a good time last night.'

'Do I?' Olive replied.

'I can see he kissed you this time.'

'Not your business, Angela.'

'Wedding bells would be.'

'Please mind your own business, Angela,' Olive repeated hurriedly, wishing no conclusion to be jumped to.

She walked out with her dogs and unlocked the doors of the Fiesta, and was approached by Denis Wilks.

'Good morning, Denis. Aren't you starting early today?'

'I was hoping to catch you, Miss.'

'Is something wrong?'

'I'm giving in my notice.'

'Oh but I don't want you to do that!'

'No more do I. But things aren't the same. I'm going to live with my sister. She's a widow, she's on her own now, and she's old, like me – we'll be company for each other, though we have had our differences. I'll be better with her than I am with that there Peter.'

'I don't know how I'll manage without you in your cottage, Denis.'

'That's it. I could say the same.'

'Can we talk later? Can I look in at Shepherd's Cottage at six-thirtyish?'

'You do that, Miss.'

She drove to work. The ups and downs of her life made concentration difficult. At midday she was again called to the telephone in Reception to speak to Martin.

They swapped thanks for the previous evening, she in as heartfelt tones as she could summon within earshot of half a dozen pet-owners, he in a more restrained form than he wished because he knew their conversation was only partially private.

Then he said: 'The bad news is that I've got to go to Cornwall for a few more days.'

'Oh Martin!'

'It's frustrating, but you know where I'd prefer to be, don't you?'

'I hope so.'

'Can't I ring you at home?'

'No – don't.'

'Ring me in an emergency, won't you? Ring my mother or the firm – somebody will know how to reach me. I'll be away for four or five days, and would love to meet as soon as I'm back. Please say you would!'

'Yes.'

'Are you all right?'

'Oh yes. Are you?'

'Yes – fine – never better – thanks to you.'

'No – it's the other way round.'

She got through the rest of her working day in a dreamy state. Her memories of Martin's kisses in the night, outside the restaurant and in his car, were wonderful. Of course she adored him, but she could not accept that he cared for her as she cared for him, because she was sure she did not deserve him. Then she remembered the nothings he had whispered in her ear that meant everything: could she be lucky after all, the luckiest person alive?

Shot through such reveries were reminders that Denis was deserting her, she would have neither Denis nor Martin to call upon and to be her defenders, and colder waves of fear of the future seemed to swamp her.

She drove home and knocked on Denis's door.

He opened it and led her into the sitting-room, which was empty except for two kitchen chairs and umpteen packing-cases and bundles tied with string.

'What does it mean, Denis? When do you think you're going?'

'Tomorrow afternoon, Miss. I've got Jim Tucker in the village driving me in his van.'

'That's so soon.'

'Can't be helped. I've left the cottage clean and Bristol fashion.'

'You and Mrs Wilks always kept it spotless. Is it Peter, is he the reason you're leaving?'

'He tried to burn down the garden shed – I caught him with the petrol I use for mowing.'

'I didn't know.'

'And my lawn will never be right in my lifetime.'

'I'm doing my best to get rid of Peter.'

'He'll be the death of someone before he lets go of The Old Hundred.'

'Oh no, don't say that! Dear Denis, I'll see about your money. But I owe you more than I can give you for all your years of looking after me and my family.'

'I was never after the money.'

'That's the truth – all the same I'll talk to Tyndall and East and see what can be done.'

When she named Martin's firm, she heard her voice softening tenderly over the single syllable East, and she began to cry.

'Miss, you stop now or you'll get me started.'

'What time is Jim Tucker coming to fetch you tomorrow?'

'Three o'clock.'

'I'll be here to say goodbye, Denis.'

'I'd appreciate it, Miss. Your family's always been good to me.'

Olive went indoors.

Angela greeted her and said: 'Sweetie, what's the matter? What's he done to you now?'

'It's Denis, he's done nothing, he couldn't do anything bad, he's packing up and retiring.'

'Oh well, you'll find another gardener.'

'You don't understand – Denis has been my family's friend for as long as I remember – and it's your Peter who's forced him to go.'

'Come on, sweetie, that's naughty. Peggy's told

122

me Denis has wanted to retire for years. Anyway, I've a bit of good news for you – Peter's landed a job on that building site, he'll begin to turn an honest penny tomorrow.'

'Will it make him more agreeable to live with?'

'Give him a chance, love! He'd be much better with you if you gave him half a chance.'

'Angela, I'm going upstairs, I want to be by myself.'

'Hang on a minute! Is Denis vacating his cottage?'

'Why? Peter can't have it, if that's what you're thinking.'

'But if Peter sticks at his job and pulls himself together, wouldn't you consider letting it to him? That way you wouldn't have him casting sheep's eyes at you and getting under your feet.'

'You present him in a flattering light.'

'Well, mothers do, don't they?'

'Sorry, Angela – I won't have Peter in Shepherd's Cottage at any price.'

'No – I'm not surprised – hard lines, Peter! Trouble is, it's a temptation. We'll have to hope he won't get tempted and turn himself into a squatter.'

Four days passed. Denis had departed. Shepherd's Cottage was empty. Olive had not heard from Martin and was convincing herself that, for him, Cornwall was synonymous with second thoughts. Peter seemed worse than ever now that he returned to The Old Hundred in the evening in filthy boots, stained trousers, torn T-shirts and brick dust on his face and in his hair.

Olive was sorry that she had no mobile phone for communication with Martin, was not even aware if he had one, and wished she was not so old-fashioned. She had never wanted to speak to him on The Old Hundred line and probably be overheard, while, in Reception at the Surgery, her responses to his calls were pathetically inhibited. But the telephone in Shepherd's Cottage was in her name, she had paid Denis's telephone bill, and could speak there in privacy. As soon as she realised she had the means to talk to Martin freely, she was torn between desire to do so and realisation that she could not. She was no feminist, she had to wait for her lover to confirm his love. In addition, she was loath to be thought unladylike by his mother, or to have to give herself away to his secretary.

Saturday arrived – still no sign of life from Martin – and Olive's general apprehensiveness intensified. Shepherd's Cottage had not yet been tampered with, nothing was more ominous than usual at home; but everything struck her as out of order. At last she lifted the telephone in the cottage and dialled the number of Tyndall and East: it was closed – she left no message on the answerphone.

Peter was working overtime. Olive did not work at weekends and joined Angela for lunch. The conversation took an alarming turn, it was really a monologue.

Angela said: 'Peter's sex-starved, that's his problem – and it's a problem most mothers can't solve. His job may keep him out of mischief, but he's mixing with other boys who talk of nothing but fornication. He's getting more pent up. He'd probably be an ordinary decent bloke if he could just find an outlet for you know what. Men are a nightmare unless they're up and doing, and equally if they can't do it, but, if they can and are, once the shouting's over they're mice, mice or kittens. Women are made to be raped, and so long as they're not bullied or murdered they have to grin and bear it. I'd hang cruel rapists – what's the point of keeping them alive? But rape without cruelty is a hard crime to prove – it's love-life for a lot of women. They should think of England instead of making a fuss.'

'That's awful talk, I hate it,' Olive said.

'Sorry, love – nursing's apt to make you call a spade a bloody shovel.'

The day dragged on for Olive. She walked her dogs, and in the evening listened to Monteverdi's *Return of Ulysses*, which tied in with her situation, collected food and took it upstairs, read Shakespeare's *Sonnets*, and eventually put out her light.

She was woken by engines, car and motorbike engines. It was ten past midnight. Her bedroom looked over the garden, but she guessed what was happening on the gravel sweep – Peter had brought back his mates after the pubs closed. The noise downstairs, raucous cries, stamping

125

feet, incomprehensible bumps, sounded like invasion.

She was paralysed with fear, fear mixed with anger. Time brought no change – they were being noisier and drinking more. She heard Angela screaming at them, she was telling them not to open bottles of wine, probably her late husband's best bottles, her stepdaughter's father's best, and ordering people out, out, but with no effect.

After however long it was – she had been incapable of turning on a light – she heard steps on the stairs, heavy energetic steps along with more vicious yelling. Men were outside her door, talking, egging each other on, their voices loud and thick with drink and their speech slurred. Somebody knocked. Her dogs were barking.

'Solly Olly, wanna' wor' – one little wor', Olly!'

The knocks continued, and Peter repeated his wants, his insults, threats and blood-curdling promises in a hateful refrain – 'Don' you tur' your nose up at me, Olly ... You're no be'er than other wom'n, not where it fu'ing ma'ers, you aren't no be'er than a fu'ing slag ... Le' me in, Olly, I'll gi' you a thr'll like you've ne'er know' ... We're comin' in, Olly, me and my frien's are go'in to do you one at a ti'!'

Angela was out there, trying to silence Peter – 'Shut up, will you shut up, you clot!' There was a moment of relative silence and confabulation. She then knocked on the door, and asked if Olive could hear her.

'You must be able to hear. And you must listen. Peter wants to talk to you for two minutes, that's all. I'll stand by while he's with you, so you won't come to any harm. Please open your door and let him in. If you don't, I'm afraid I can't answer for the consequences.'

Olive held her breath.

Soon the hubbub began again. Peter was barging against her door, and yelling a phrase that included the word 'mur'er'. Angela's voice rose shrilly above his.

'Stop it! If you break in she'll have the law on you. Stop it or finish in prison! Go downstairs, all of you, and leave this house at once! Out – you've done enough harm – go, go!'

They obeyed her unexpectedly. The house was quiet, but the raised voices were not far away. At last engines revved up and vehicles skidded over the gravel and roared into the distance.

Olive slept no more. She cried and yearned for Martin and made plans. Soon after it was light she crept downstairs. Angela had cleared up – there were no instantly visible signs of damage. Olive let herself and her dogs out by the back door and entered Shepherd's Cottage.

It was intact and empty – she had been afraid of finding Peter's cronies encamped there and vomit on the floor. Denis had left it clean and tidy, and the furnishings provided by the Crightons years ago were still in place, the double bed upstairs, sheets and blankets, crockery, cutlery and the two kitchen chairs in the sitting-room.

Later, when she returned to the house, she met Angela and said: 'I'm moving into Denis's cottage.'

'Really?'

'I'm only going to sleep there – I'm not evicting myself or being evicted from The Old Hundred.'

'Are you cross about last night?'

'Cross isn't the word.'

'Well, I'm sorry the lads got a bit too excited. But, if I may say so, sweetie, I don't think you played your cards right. Peter's silly about you, but you could have taken the wind out of his sails easily.'

'No thanks – I know what you're suggesting! If he molests me or lifts a finger against me, I'll call the police and lodge a complaint. I have a telephone available in Shepherd's Cottage, which wasn't the case here – I couldn't get to the telephone here.'

'I'm going to miss you, love.'

'The house still belongs to me, Angela.'

'I'm well aware of that.'

Throughout the rest of the day she carried belongings across to the cottage – Peter did not show his face and sneaked off somewhere on his motorbike. She also persuaded Jim Tucker to come and fix bolts to the cottage doors and windows. Against her will and better judgment, she yielded to Angela's urgings to share a midday meal, and then to collect her supper, as she had been doing recently – she was still paying for the food. She fled from her home with her supper tray, and in due course, after the dogs had been out for the last time, locked herself into her fastness.

The deed was done. But now it occurred to her that she might not be able to do it for long. From there it was only a short step to wondering if she had been cowardly and rash. She lay in Denis's bed and thought of Martin, and every terror but one subsided. The one that racked her was that Martin would think she had done the wrong thing, and she sobbed herself to sleep.

The next morning, Monday morning, she realised that she would not get in to work – she again had to apologise to Tim Spell for letting him down.

She had breakfast in Shepherd's Cottage, tea and toast, but no post – she had forgotten about possible letters from Martin in the panic of yesterday. Moreover she could not wash her hands of The Old Hundred, she would have to keep watch on it and especially its inmates.

She entered by the back door as soon as she thought Peter would have gone to his job. Letters for her lay on the table in the hall, but not the one she had hoped for.

Peter came downstairs. She shrivelled inside, she had not set eyes on him since he besieged her in her bedroom. She cursed herself for trespassing in her own house at the wrong time. But he was in a hurry, only said in passing, 'Hi, Olly – no wakey-wakey t'day,' and went out through the front door, which he slammed.

The spirit of rebellion stirred in her again,

and depressed her further. How dare Peter come down her stairs as if he owned the place, and why did he go out by the front door while she crept in through the back? She could not sit down and submit to the insolence and injustice, and nothing would induce her to lie down.

Angela appeared, and confused Olive by smiling at what were meant to be frowns.

'Were you all right in your sanctuary last night?' she asked.

'Yes, thanks.'

'I worried about you.'

'Well, I felt safer there than here.'

'I'm hoping you'll be back where you belong soon. Peter's penitent, although he's hopeless at expressing himself, and he might go into lodgings if he hangs on to his job. We're both impatient to cut the cord, if you catch my meaning.'

'He'll be late for work today.'

'I know. He's so stupid! But I don't think him as bad as you do. How could I?'

'I'll be staying in Shepherd's Cottage for the foreseeable future.'

'Where will you eat? I hope you don't intend to spurn me and my cooking. I'd hate it if we stopped speaking to each other – honestly, love, I couldn't abide it.'

'No – if you're prepared to cook something in the evenings, I'll be grateful.'

'It's the least I can do. You're feeding us, for goodness' sake, you're our hostess, when all's said. What about lunch, for instance today? You can't be going to the Surgery.'

'All right, Angela.'

'Is that yes or no? Do have lunch with me! I'm roasting a chicken, and I've picked peas from your own garden to go with it.'

'Thanks again. I've got to be here today to organise the changes.'

'Can I help?'

'No, thanks. See you later!'

Olive walked with her dogs to the council cottage where Peggy and Joe Williams lived.

The affectionate preliminaries led into her account of the previous weekend, the Saturday night assault on her home and virtue, and her flight on Sunday to Shepherd's Cottage.

Peggy's reactions were unintentionally discouraging, although they could have been predicted.

'You can't live there, Miss. You're entitled to live in your own proper place.'

Olive had to describe the steps that had led to Shepherd's Cottage.

'Oh they have been pests to you,' Peggy commented. 'That Angela's got a foxy side, although she's pleasant enough to speak to, and Peter, he wants to be seen to. What's happened to Mr East?'

Olive cried. She could not stop herself.

She spoke through tears: 'I don't know. I wish I knew. But I must struggle on, Peg. Who's going to do Denis's work?'

'You won't find a handyman like Denis in the village. I'm sorry he packed up so sudden, I told him he shouldn't, but what with Peter and his age it was no use, and he was being pressed by his sister.'

131

'I can't let everything go to pot. I don't know what I can and can't afford. The Old Hundred's turned into my millstone – I used to love it so!'

'Poor Miss!'

'No – I'm not that – I don't deserve pity.'

'I'll clean the cottage for you, I will.'

'Thank you for your kindness, Peg – but Denis left it spick and span. Should I ask Jim Tucker about a new Denis?'

'That'd be best.'

Olive's search for male support of her ownership of The Old Hundred occupied most of the rest of the day. She thought of, she yearned in vain for, Martin, while she traipsed from Peggy to Jim Tucker, then to the home of a man who lived in the village of Benton and was recommended by Jim, then to another recommended man who lived along the road to Chippenham, and finally when she despaired of finding any member of the opposite sex willing to lend her his hand.

She returned to Shepherd's Cottage. Tea revived her somewhat, and that unwonted rebelliousness pointed the remnants of her energy in a different direction. Instead of inwardly and sometimes outwardly whimpering, she judged Martin severely, although still willing to listen to what he might have to say in his defence. He should not have thrown her to the wolves in the shape of two Malones, he had not stood by his word that he would protect her; but the rider to her criticisms was that she now had cause not to wait patiently for his summons. Furthermore, she had reason to contact Tyndall and East in order to talk about Denis's farewell gift, and a telephone was at her disposal.

She rang the number of Martin's home in Warminster and prepared to leave a message with his mother.

He answered the telephone.

He recognised her voice, quavering as it was, and exclaimed with enthusiasm: 'This is telepathy. I have my diary in my hand, open at the page with your number on it. I was going to try to ring you in spite of knowing how difficult it is for you to speak at home and at work. I arrived five minutes ago – Cornwall stretched out from day to day and even from hour to hour, and I had to keep on delaying a letter to you or a postcard. I'm sorry! Can we meet? When can we meet?'

8

Their conversation did not end there. It continued for half an hour. She had to own up that
she was not in The Old Hundred, and why, and
all the rest of it. She expected him at least to
convey an impression that he disapproved; but
he sympathised with her ordeal and was the
more concerned for her safety.

In reply to the question that concluded every
chapter of her accidents and vicissitudes, he
replied that she must do nothing that could
compromise her legal position.

'Ideally, you shouldn't move back to The Old
Hundred – if you did you'd be condoning the
actions of Angela and Peter Malone, and the law
would rule that you therefore had no grounds
for complaint.'

'But I looked in to collect my mail this morning, I had lunch there, and I've said I'll collect
my supper that Angela's cooking now – I gave
up eating with the Malones in the evenings long
ago.'

'But you still pay the bills for housekeeping,
don't you?'

'Yes – they go to your Mr Stewart, who re-
imburses Angela for anything she's paid for – my

father arranged for Mr Stewart to manage the money matters on my behalf.'

'Better not let the Malones pay for things which might benefit you. Can you cope for a few more days? I'm talking to Robin Tanner first thing tomorrow – Robin knows more about your sort of problem than I do. Don't worry that I'll hustle you into a law court! I'm doing my best not to hustle you in any way. I'm a cautious person who would nonetheless love to see you soon, if possible.'

She laughed and mentioned Denis's gift which she was planning to discuss with Mr Stewart.

'When would you like to do that?'

'Well – tomorrow, if Mr Stewart has time.'

'Shall I fix it for midday?'

'Yes, please.'

'Would you have lunch with me afterwards?'

'I'd love to,' she said.

The next day – eventually, as both parties viewed the hours that intervened – Martin and Olive – without her dogs – met and drove in his Rover to the picturesque pub in Stonefield.

The sun again shone on them, the stream purled near their bench-seat in the garden, and Martin said before they began to eat that he now had something to tell her. She was afraid of what might come next, and blushed shyly, then was surprised.

He said: 'I want to give you an autobiographical thumbnail sketch. Would you mind? I'm thirty-one, healthy to the best of my knowledge, in work, a company director, comfortably off and the sole heir of my mother – I was an only child, too. I'm domesticated, I think, and I'm certain that I'm not ambitious – I don't want to be famous and I'd hate to rule the world. But you're probably waiting to hear a bit more about my emotional history. For nine years I was attached to a girl who wouldn't marry me, and we called it a day eighteen months ago. I haven't messed around much, I'm a romantic, I'm still a romantic, and there it is or there I am.'

'Can I ask you why your romance went wrong? Don't say if you'd rather not!'

'She was a career girl, another lawyer, and against encumbrances like a husband and children. We never fell out, we fizzled out, "parted amicably", as jargon puts it, and we don't keep in touch, though we'd be quite friendly in the unlikely event of our meeting – she lives and works in London. It's well and truly over. That's all, except to repeat that I'm nine years older than you are.'

'It doesn't matter,' she said.

'Thank you for saying so,' he replied.

'I've got so little to tell,' she volunteered. But he waited, and she resumed: 'I'm afraid I never altogether grew up although I'm twenty-two. Until my mother died, I was wrapped up in her – and for us it was all music and books. I didn't go to many children's parties, and loved animals. I suppose psychologists would find something wrong with me, but I don't think they'd be right – they are so often wrong, aren't they?'

'They are.'

'Do you love music? Are you interested in opera?'

'Yes to your first question – I love classical music but don't listen to it as much as I'd like to. Opera's passed me by and I wish it hadn't.'

'If you're open-minded, you'd love opera. We felt, my mother and then I felt, that something Tosca sings in Puccini's opera was our signature tune – she sings that she has lived for love and art. It's a beautiful aria, but really it was silly of us to identify with those sentiments, because my mother wasn't in love with my father, not romantically, and I had very little experience of any love except for animals. Lots of women feel the same way about that aria, I believe.'

'Have you got a recording of *Tosca*?'

'Oh yes.'

'Will you play it for me some time?'

'Yes.'

'Olive...'

'Yes?'

'Has anything I've said jarred on you?'

'No – the opposite. Do I jar on you?'

'Not at all.'

They smiled at each other, those easy conspiratorial smiles of mutual approval and attraction.

'Lucky we're going to eat cold food,' he remarked, and they both laughed. 'I've got one other thing to tell you,' he added.

'Pleasant or unpleasant?'

'We'll see. Robin Tanner has spoken. His

137

short-term solution of your problem would be to lodge a legally drawn up complaint with the police and ease yourself back into The Old Hundred together with a protective male resident. Longer term, he's sure the Malones will blot their own copybook and get themselves in serious trouble.'

'I can't follow his advice – yours was not to move back, and I liked it better.'

'The difference between his and mine is that I would have offered to be the male protector.'

'Oh – thank you – but I'm not ready – I couldn't...'

'Say no more.'

'I'm sorry. And I don't want to be involved with the police or the law.'

'For the time being, in that case, you'll have to depend on me to rush to your rescue. I've finished with Cornwall, I'm not going anywhere, and my hope is that you'll realise the object of my existence – romantically speaking – is to be of service to you.'

'Oh Martin!'

'Now I'll allow you to eat your lunch.'

They made a plan to meet again before saying goodbye with a daytime kiss.

In the course of the next ten days they met three times for lunch and once for a woodland walk after work and before supper. They were very happy, but could have been more so. She bloomed because of Martin and shivered because of the Malones, and his joys were diluted by anxiety on her account. She also wondered to what extent she was motivated by requiring professional attention, while he was possibly wondering if he was the only available straw for her to clutch at. Their romance was haunted by the Malones, and the sunlit prospect they thought they could see ahead was overshadowed by the stocky outline of Angela and the overbearing bulk of Peter.

She refused Martin's invitations to have dinner with him again, for instance at the place where they had danced, and she did not invite him even to see how she lived in Shepherd's Cottage. She did not trust either of them not to overstep the mark in her mind, and her circumstances were restrictive. Nothing was settled, she was unsettled, she did not want to love him absent-mindedly, she was not ready, as she had said.

The invitation she did accept was to lunch on a Sunday with his mother. Her friendship with Mrs East added to her confidence in Martin, and her visit to the calm and well-run house in Warminster was a bitter-sweet reminder of The Old Hundred as it had been, might be, and was not.

She was spending as little time as possible there. She was in and out for her mail before the Malones stirred, and in the evenings, although Peter was clearly no keener to see her than she was to see him, if for different reasons, she cut short her chat with Angela and ran away with her tray.

One evening Angela said in a tone of

exasperation: 'Olive, isn't this ducking and diving ridiculous?'

'What do you mean?' Olive countered to gain time.

'Well, you're not in danger – Peter's been sober night after night, he's more frightened of you than you need to be of him – and it's so uncomfortable for you, having to cross the yard for supper – and for me, because you behave as if we've quarrelled, which isn't true.'

'I can't share a house with Peter. I haven't been bitten once, I've been bitten more often than that. That's all there is to it.'

'But we were friends – I'm still your friend – and you've become unfriendly towards me. I shouldn't be in the dock because of Peter's offences.'

'And I can't argue the point, Angela. Things could change but actions speak louder than words.'

'Do you want Peter to grovel at your feet?'
'No!'

'He's working hard, he's a grown man, he hasn't had your advantages – you can't expect him to be diplomatic.'

'You make very light of the things that have happened here in these last months. I can't enumerate them, I don't want a row. We'd better try to live and let live for the present.'

'All right. As you wish. But it's sad, it's no fun, and I may decide to call it a day and go elsewhere. If so you'll have to make arrangements with Peter – he won't listen to his mother.'

'That's blackmail, Angela.'

'No, no – it's common sense – but I won't do anything in a hurry – you'll come round in the end.'

This conversation caused Olive a sleepless night and provoked her to share her despondency with Martin over lunch on the following day.

'Angela's trying to lure me into The Old Hundred, and knows I won't return so long as Peter's in residence. She holds out an olive branch – a false olive branch – and I refuse to accept it. She justifies herself and at once puts me in the wrong. She'd actually like to be rid of me altogether. I'm not being melodramatic, I'm almost convinced that it's life or death – I really am – nothing in between.'

'I won't let it get as lethal as that. The moment's not far off when I tackle her.'

'I hope she won't get round you. She gets round everybody, men especially. She's so plausible. She never seems to be hot under the collar. She's utterly amoral, and has a one-track mind.'

'We'll win the last battle.'

'Will we?' she responded with a faint ring of confidence.

A day or two later an event changed the balance of the conflict.

Olive was due to have lunch with Martin in Warminster. She had agreed to because she was not very busy at the Surgery and he was busy in his office, and besides she had shopping to do. She parked the Fiesta early, walked to the shops,

141

and turned towards the offices of Tyndall and
East, where they were to meet. She took a quiet
detour, through run-down and misnamed
Harmony Street, and passed a dusty antique
shop with a desk in the window.

An idea arrested her. She retraced her steps
and peered through the window of the shop.
She could not be certain, but the desk looked
like the one in the study at The Old Hundred,
her father's desk, at which he had spent a large
proportion of his working life. She caught her
breath or uttered an involuntary sob. She was
afraid to be wrong, to confront the shopkeeper
and be wrong – anyway Martin would be waiting for her.

She met him outside his office building – he
was standing on the pavement. His first reaction
to her story was to dart back to his office to
fetch a tape recorder, the small dictaphone type.
Then they hurried to Harmony Street, while he
recorded the date, time, their names, where they
were, where they were going and why. The shop
was called Antique Trading, its window was
dirty, its interior dark, and the desk was of a
higher quality than the other visible items.

'Is it yours?' Martin asked.

'I'm sure it is,' Olive replied.

'How sure is sure?'

'Ninety per cent.'

'Let's go in! Will you leave the talking to me?'

'Willingly.'

They entered, ringing a bell attached to the
door. A middle-aged unkempt man emerged

from the back parts – he wore two pieces of a three-piece suit, grubby trousers and waistcoat, no jacket. Greetings were exchanged.

Martin said: 'We like the desk in the window.'

'It's a fine one, Chippendale kneehole type,' the man informed them.

'Is it expensive?'

'It is, very.'

'How expensive?'

'I'd take two thousand for a quick sale. It'll go to London and cost a lot more there.'

'We'd have to know its provenance, of course.'

'I couldn't give you that information unless I had the seller's permission. And he's abroad at present – it would take time to contact him, he might or might not oblige, and the price of the item would rise along with the delay. I need a quick sale because I had to borrow to buy the desk.'

'Are you the owner of the shop?'

'In a manner of speaking. May I ask if you're private or trade?'

'Private. We couldn't decide to buy immediately. Do you have a card with your telephone number?'

'Yes, sir.'

'Thank you. Are you Mr Beake?'

'I am. Would you like to take a closer look at the desk?'

'In a manner of speaking, as you say, Mr Beake. Can you guarantee that it's not stolen property?'

143

'Who are you?'

'This lady might be the owner.'

'Oh no! I bought it in good faith. You're not the lady the lads said they were acting for? I've been conned, madam – I don't deal in stolen goods on purpose.'

'Will you tell us the truth? I've recorded our conversation so far. You'd benefit by coming clean, Mr Beake.'

'Well, you've played a dirty trick to start with, recording me without warning.'

'What did you pay for the desk?'

'Five hundred.'

'Wasn't that a dirty price? Who were these lads?'

'Don't know. They spun me a yarn... You can have the desk back if it's yours, madam – I don't want trouble.'

'Would you identify the lads?'

'If I could. The one who did the talking was called Pete.'

'Okay, Mr Beake. We'll go away and double-check. There's obviously been some criminal activity, whoever the desk rightfully belongs to. Whether or not we pr ss charges or inform the police is another matter. Good afternoon.'

Outside in the street Martin said to Olive: 'You mustn't pity that nasty little crook.'

She said: 'I don't. But I am grateful. Somebody else has made the mistake this time.'

Ten minutes later, over lunch at an Italian

restaurant close to Martin's office, he asked: 'Is it your father's? Is it yours?'

'Yes,' she answered. 'It's got the O for Olive that I scratched on one of the drawers when I was a child.'

They discussed what to do next and agreed that they should confront Angela without delay. But, Olive then pointed out, after the confrontation her relationship with her stepmother would be altered to an insupportable degree. And Martin allowed that it could be impossible for her to live within striking distance of the Malones after accusing them of theft and trying to put Peter in prison.

On the other hand, contrarily, they agreed that they had to do something, they must react to the crime that had been committed, and that they had probably been presented with the means to the end they wished for.

She said: 'I only want them to go, nothing else.'

Martin suggested that if the worst came to the worst she could stay with his mother: 'She'd love a visit from you – and my flat's separate, I wouldn't be in your way.'

They drove in their own cars to The Old Hundred and parked on the gravel sweep. Olive was relieved to see no sign of Peter's motorbike, and Martin rang the doorbell.

Angela admitted them. She retained her poise, she smiled and wished to know to what she owed the pleasure, although she must have realised that she was more likely to suffer pain in the near future.

'Can I give you a cup of tea or coffee? Come into the sitting-room.'

Martin said: 'It's the study we're interested in Angela.'

'Oh that! Yes, well, your call's not altogether unexpected. It had to happen, I suppose. Help yourself to a look!'

They did so. The space where the desk had stood was bare. They all adjourned to the sitting-room.

Martin began: 'The antique dealer who bought the desk has spilled the beans and would give evidence against your son. Peter's committed a crime, and you're his accomplice. Theoretically we could instigate legal proceedings against you.'

'Only if Olive agreed,' Angela said. 'Would you do that to us, Olive?'

'It's the house,' Olive replied. 'I can't go on sharing the house with you.'

'Sharing? You've chosen not to share of your own free will.'

'Freedom didn't come into it, Angela. You know Peter forced me out. He threatened me, he threatened to do bad things, he and his gang – you were there, you were on their side.'

'I know that's your story.'

'It's not a story, it's true.'

'Have you got witnesses, sweetie?'

'Peter himself –'

'Excuse me, Peter loves and respects you. He's unhappy that you've taken against him. He wouldn't harm you, you or me, for the world.'

Martin interrupted: 'What progress are you

making towards finding separate accommodation for yourself? The will of Sir James gives an impression that he expected you to stay at The Old Hundred temporarily.'

'Progress is nil, I'm sorry to say, Martin. Olive knows that the money left to me was mostly swallowed up by debts. I was in deeper water financially than James knew – I didn't tell him, I didn't want to worry him. If I had the money I would have spent it on buying back James's desk – but no such luck. I suppose I might be able to rustle up a down payment on a one-roomed flat somewhere and then set to work on paying off a mortgage. I tried to follow your instructions alone those lines, Martin, but when I was seeking paid work Olive begged me to come back to The Old Hundred – didn't you, sweetie? I have had a shot at earning my living since I became a widow, but Olive wouldn't have it.'

'Are you aiming to live here permanently? Is that your aim?'

'Oh I don't know – I don't have aims, Martin – I can't afford aims – I just live from hand to mouth and hope for the best. But my Peter may be needing money for fines and what-not, so I'm glad I haven't spent every last penny of mine on housing. I've obeyed my husband and taken some responsibility for my son by staying at The Old Hundred – is that wrong?'

'Bailing out your son is nothing to do with Sir James' intentions. And I think a court of law would think your interpretation of his will offended against natural justice.'

147

'Good heavens, Martin, what's more natural than love between a mother and her child? Peter's not wicked, he's weak. He was tempted by all the valuable furniture and things lying around in this house – the value of any one item was beyond his dreams. He took what nobody else seemed to want, and when I found out and scolded him he couldn't see why a poor person shouldn't benefit a little from another person's wealth – I've always told him Robin Hoods go to prison these days.'

Olive said: 'How can you suggest that my father's desk meant nothing to me? It has sentimental value apart from what it's worth. My family worked hard to buy its furniture.'

'But you didn't guard your treasures, did you, love? You abandoned them. Peter's simple-minded, he thought you didn't care.'

Martin intervened: 'Angela, you've been lucky in my opinion, and now I believe the time has come to tie up loose ends and strike a deal. Peter's in trouble, both of you are, and Olive's in trouble of another kind. A swap, an exchange of acts of generosity and goodwill, would be practical.'

'Are you saying no prosecution in return for our making ourselves scarce?'

'Roughly, yes.'

'No go, Martin. I've been too generous already. It's won me nothing but ingratitude.'

Olive exclaimed: 'What are you talking about?' and Martin chimed in: 'That's an original point of view.'

'Your father, Olive love, your father was determined to leave The Old Hundred and its contents, and enough money to keep it up, to me. Yes, he was dead set on cutting you out. He loved me so much, and I'm sure he loved you, but you always made him feel awkward, you and your mother looked down on him, he felt. But I wouldn't steal from you. I told him straight that nothing much was his to leave as he wished, because I knew he'd married money, the house and all had belonged to Lady C., your mother, sweetie, and was yours by rights. When there's talk of kicking me into the gutter, and prosecuting Peter, I can't swallow it, I won't swallow it, and that's where we are today. You're here by the grace of me, not vice versa, and Peter's pinched something, one of the many things that might have been his, but for me. You think you're hard done by, but the true truth is that you've got off light so far. The deal is simpler than you imagined, Martin. I can't see myself leaving The Old Hundred in a hurry, so you and Olive have to go away and think of new answers to the old questions. What's changed isn't an old desk, it's the story of my husband's will and its effects. And I have a witness to what James had in mind, a gentleman in your profession, Martin, a colleague of yours, Mr Harris.'

They beat a retreat as strategically as they could. Olive and Martin were not defeated, the war was not over, but they had been ambushed.

Angela had not only caught them out by claiming she might have inherited The Old Hundred and that she was the unselfish and generous one, but had also succeeded in wounding Olive severely.

The cars, the Fiesta and the Rover, pulled into the verge on the Luffield-Warminster road. The drivers had agreed to meet out of sight of Angela and before they went their separate ways, Martin to his office and Olive to the Surgery.

Olive was glad to have the chance to cry privately on Martin's shoulder.

'It can't be true, can it?' she sobbed. 'My father wouldn't have disinherited me – I know he wouldn't – he wasn't as uneasy with me as she made out – and it would have been against all his principles and his character to steal Mummy's property and possessions and to want to hand them over to his nurse, even if she had become his wife.'

'I'm sure it was lies from start to finish.'

'But she says Mr Harris is ready to bear witness that Daddy wanted to leave me nothing.'

'Mr Harris is a rogue. He has a bad name in the legal profession. He may be our white hope, because I don't think he'd dare to perjure himself.'

'What are we to do, Martin?'

'Well, whatever we decide to do must be done in a hurry, before we accept the theft of the desk and surrender unconditionally. I suggest we get a full inventory taken of the contents of the Old Hundred, and I talk to the police. We should do more than that, but I'm reluctant to create a situation that virtually exiles you from your home.'

'I feel I'm stuck with them for ever.'

'Don't despair. The law can't be such an ass as to offer you no means of recovering your property. I'll have to have further words with Robin Tanner. Meanwhile, would you be ready to go ahead with an inventory?'

'What would it entail?'

'You'd have to sign a letter, which I'll write, giving me leave to organise the inventory. I'll also write to Angela to say when it will happen. I'm afraid you'd need to show the people taking the inventory the whereabouts of everything. But it's essential if we're to stop the Malones popping items as they please.'

'I suppose I must. She was so inconsiderate today – I don't know how she could have concocted those hateful stories about my family.'

'And you won't mind if I seek advice from the police?'

'Oh dear! You'd better not ask me, Martin. I trust you to be sensible and sensitive.'

He thanked her. He kissed her. He said he would bring the letter for her to sign to the Surgery early the next morning.

Then he asked: 'What about tonight? Where will you feel safe? Don't forget my mother.'

'I won't leave Shepherd's Cottage empty for Peter to squat in. I won't be driven out.'

'Are you sure?'

'Certain!'

151

At length they parted company.

Olive, as the day progressed, was increasingly nervous of returning to Old Hundred territory, in which Angela now seemed to have a proprietorial interest. She extended her evening walk with Buddy and Whisper. She sat in the Fiesta, imagining what she might have let herself in for. Martin was no doubt right to think in terms of inventories and recourse to the law; but he did not have to face Angela within minutes, to be reproached by her or floored by her long-suffering amiability, or to await an encounter with the criminal who was likely to want to express his opinion of her plan to get him arrested.

Her courage dissolved kaleidoscopically into a new pattern, the pattern of guilt and frailty. If there was even a grain of truth in Angela's rigmarole, she was at fault. She had to admit that her mother and she herself had possibly given her father cause to feel unappreciated and on a lower cultural level. Sadness was another debilitating factor. She was too confused about rights and wrongs, and too kind to fight against odds that were apparently and overwhelmingly against her.

Supposing Martin were physically propping her up, that might have made all the difference. Together they could perhaps succeed. But clear-headedness cut in at this point: the more she involved Martin in her legal drama, the less easy to extricate herself from him in a loving context. Extrication was not on her mind, the very opposite was the case; nevertheless she could see the error of swearing to love a man for ever because he was performing the duties of a solicitor to her satisfaction. She had to wait until the legal business was settled, no longer in the picture, before she could invite Martin to be her protector in every sense.

She braced herself at last and drove home. It was suppertime – she entered the house and found Angela in the kitchen.

Immediately Angela apologised. She did not deny her story or withdraw it, but regretted the facts that she had said more than she meant to, that their friendship was taking such a muddling and miserable turn, and completely understood why Olive had sought the advice of Martin when she found her own desk for sale in a shop window.

Olive said she was sorry, too – but was not proud of the ambiguity and feebleness of her response.

They were reconciled within the limits of politeness and vigilance. Olive accepted her tray of appetising food, took it across to the cottage and rang Martin at home.

'I can't go through with it,' she said. 'I'm being stupid, I expect, but I've had second thoughts – it looks as if I'm going to have to live with Angela and Peter for ages – and I've just seen her and we can't exist at close quarters with daggers drawn.'

'Did she explain herself? Was she contrite?'

'Not really – she was sort of sorry – but... Please understand!'

'I do. I thought you might not be ready to fight a war. I'll suspend operations until further notice. Are you all right?'

'Yes. I met Angela when I collected my supper. It's peculiar, her cooking delicious meals for me and stealing my house. She probably thinks her cooking is my rent. Thank you for being patient.'

'Good night, sleep tight!'

Olive, after eating, was overcome by fatigue. She was battle-weary, and exhausted by her sense of impending disaster. She put the dogs out at nine-thirty, and was asleep by ten.

She was woken by a noise in her bedroom. Her heart thumped, she was terrified that somebody was in her room or in the cottage. The noise sounded again – over by her window, which was wide open. She ventured out of her bed to cross the floor and trod on a stone or a bit of brick. It was Peter, he had been throwing stones at her bedroom window, and she tried not to look out, but could not fail to see him – he was shining a big torch on his own face and in her eyes.

'I got you, Olly. You been fri'ning my ma. Don' you dare fri'en Angie, you and your fancy ma'. You dare, Olly!'

She shut the window. He was still there, shouting at her and now making a gesture with his finger. She trembled and shook, and wove her way back to bed.

He threw more stones at her windowpanes, and continued to shout and swear for some

154

minutes. Even when he went away she could not stop trembling – she was in the grip of her reflexes, mindless and ice-cold.

An hour or two later, round about three o'clock, she had recovered her power of thought, and had changed her mind again.

9

She rang Martin at eight, she could not wait any longer.

He listened to her and said: 'Leave everything to me. You can't go on like this. Be at Shepherd's Cottage at two this afternoon if you can – if you can't, ring me at the office.'

She carried her tray across to the house. Angela was in the kitchen.

Olive said: 'Peter threatened me last night.'

'He can't have, sweetie. He was here all evening, watching TV.'

'I'm not asking you, I'm telling you, Angela. He woke me and threatened me – he threatened me again. Martin's coming here to do an inventory at two o'clock this afternoon.'

'Oh well – I'd better be out of your way.'

'I think it would be much better for all of us if you were here.'

'Okay, why not? I'll see you later.'

She drove to the Surgery and obtained Tim Spell's permission to take the afternoon off. Throughout the morning she continued to be haunted by her memory of Peter's countenance illuminated in the night, the distorting shadows across it, his hostile expression and glittering eyes.

She returned at one thirty, together with a sandwich and an apple bought at a local convenience store. At two she heard motors and walked round to the front of The Old Hundred. A convoy of vehicles was pulling up on the gravel sweep, and Angela had opened the front door and was smiling a welcome as if she were the householder.

Martin had brought over a clerk with clipboard, and the antique dealer, Mr Beake. There was also a police car containing two officers, one male, the other female. The third vehicle was a van, from which two strong young men emerged. In addition, Peter roared up on his motorbike.

Everybody converged on the front door, where Martin made an announcement.

'Can you all see that I'm holding a tape recorder? I'm going to record conversations as I think fit from now on. These recordings are for reference only at present, but, if Miss Crighton should decide to press charges or if the police officers should decide to take the matter into their own hands, they could be used in a legal process. Thank you. Now, please fetch the desk!'

His instruction was directed at the men with the van. The desk was duly extracted, carried into the house and replaced in the study – the action was overseen by Martin's clerk.

The others, Olive, Martin, Angela, Peter, Mr Beake and the police officers, moved into the sitting-room.

Peter addressed Olive in an undertone: 'Meet agai', Olly!'

'Aren't you working today?' she asked.

'Stopped that, Olly – have to stay home to see you're not crue' to Angie.'

Martin took over the meeting.

'Some days ago Peter Malone stole a desk from The Old Hundred at Luffield, Wiltshire, property of Miss Olive Crighton, and sold it for five hundred pounds to Mr Ronald Beake, antique dealer of Harmony Street, Warminster – dates are available.'

Peter interrupted.

'Hang on, Marti' – I never stole, I never seen that bloke – wha' you jawing abou'?'

Angela said with resignation: 'You're behind the times, Peter,' and Mr Beake said simultaneously, pointing a shaky finger at Peter: 'He's the culprit, he got me into this mess, and I'm suing him for my five hundred smackers.'

Martin weighed in: 'Lady Crighton has admitted that her son committed the crime in question and that she was his accomplice. Lady Crighton has a right to live in The Old Hundred until she can find accommodation elsewhere, the right conferred upon her by the will of her late husband, Sir James Crighton, but whether or not that right extends to the presence in the house of her son is a question that might have to be proved in a court of law. What is beyond doubt is that Peter Malone has now revealed his criminal inclinations, by burgling Miss Crighton's house, also by harassing and persecuting Miss Crighton herself, and is therefore on borrowed time and could sooner or later be barred by law from frequenting these premises.'

Peter addressed the police officers: 'Hark at him! He fancies her, tha's the tru'. He wan's me out so he can get in. It's all porkies. You tell the tru', Olly – I never harmed you, did I?'

Martin said: 'My clerk Sam can start to take the inventory.'

They all toured the house, and it was extremely unpleasant. On the bedroom floor Peter tried to disallow entry into his room, which was strewn with dirty tea mugs and pornographic mags, and Angela was angry that he had omitted to tidy it as promised. For Olive, seeing the bed where her mother and her father died, and she had perhaps disgraced them, was an ordeal. Her own former bedroom with its beloved books, Jane Austen and Emily Brontë and the others, pierced her through and through with nostalgia.

Peter's foul stream of gutter politics polluted the atmosphere further – 'Olly's got the lot and I got no'ing, and it's not fair ... I'd be a gen'-man if she gimme one of her pictures.' Downstairs in the dining-room he called for drinks all round, whining and calling Olive a 'fu'ing bitch and meanie'. The policeman warned him to mind his language, and Martin appealed to Angela to control and restrain her son. But he still bumped heavily into Olive in doorways and mocked her with his apologies – 'I do beg your pardo', Miss!'

At length the police departed after a sharp exchange with Peter, and gave a lift back to Warminster to Sam the clerk and Mr Beake, who still muttered that he would reclaim his five hundred pounds somehow or other.

Angela accompanied Olive and Martin out of doors – Peter had vanished.

Her goodbye to Martin was frank and un-reproachful, she was or pretended to be above the embarrassment of the afternoon; and she urged Olive to look in for her supper as usual.

'We have no quarrel, love – everything will sort itself out – I'll take care of it – please let me feed you!'

Martin said to Olive: 'I've more to tell you if you'll get into my car.'

Olive did so.

'You shouldn't be alone in your cottage at night,' he said. 'I'd love to sleep there, as you know, but don't think that would suit for various reasons. Would your ex-housekeeper Peggy or her husband oblige? I remember how fond you and she were of each other.'

'I don't think even he would dare...'

'Please ask Peggy for my sake. Otherwise I'll have to spend the night in the farmyard.'

'I never meant to be such a bore...'

'Please!'

He then drove her to the cottage where Peggy and Joe lived, and waited outside until she emerged with Peggy and he received the requisite assurances.

He said: 'Sorry to have been so bossy for the last few hours. But now we'll both sleep more soundly.'

They kissed goodbye, and wished that the

160

crisis was subsiding instead of building up and that they could concentrate exclusively on each other.

Olive walked back to Shepherd's Cottage. She collected Buddy and Whisper and took them for a longer walk. She was loath to sit still. She was unable to relax, and the confrontation in store in the evening put her in a dither. She could easily skip the meal, or as easily buy something to eat and bring it home; but then she would have to speak to one or other Malone on the telephone.

At eight o'clock she crossed the yard and in The Old Hundred kitchen found herself in the company of both Malones.

It began better than expected. Angela was her polite self, and Peter expressed regret for his afternoon performance.

'Angie says I was a stupi' 'nana. Solly, Olly!'

Olive's tray was prepared. Angie invited her to stay and eat with them. When she refused, seizing her opportunity to say that Peggy was coming to sleep at the cottage, Peter said she was a bloody good for nothing cow.

Olive smiled with difficulty and made as if to leave.

Peter detained her verbally. She looked round and was alarmed by the malice in his eyes. He shouted after her as she hurried out: 'Those puppy-dogs of yours, Olly – you love your puppy-dogs – better keep a close eye on them, ha'nt you?'

*   *   *

161

Peggy arrived at Shepherd's Cottage bringing her night things in a plastic bag, and was startled to find Olive in tears.

It was the threat to her dogs, Olive explained. 'He wouldn't do that, would he? He couldn't, could he?' she demanded, crying because she feared that he could.

Peggy trotted out the conventional phrases of reassurances – 'Never! ... Don't you believe it ... He was pulling your leg ... Never mind!' – and they made up the camp bed which Olive would sleep on in the sitting-room.

'You should be upstairs, Miss,' Peggy said. 'He'd get a shock if he climbed into the cottage and found me.'

Olive would not hear of it. She was so grateful that she wanted Peggy to be comfortable. The only security precaution she agreed to take was to keep Denis's toasting fork, a stout implement with sharp prongs, on the floor by her bed. Peggy promised that she was a light sleeper, and Olive that she would shout as loudly as she could in an emergency; but both women hoped the dogs would see off an intruder.

The night passed peacefully. At seven-thirty Peggy left to cook breakfast for Joe, and at eight or thereabouts Olive summoned up her courage and returned her supper tray to the kitchen of The Old Hundred.

Angie was there, blessedly without Peter, who could again sleep late now he was unemployed.

Angie was all smiles, according to her practice. She asked if Olive had slept well, and said that she herself had slept like a top. Then she asked Olive not to rush away, and referred to the events of the previous afternoon.

'I see why you had to have an inventory – but Peter's Peter and that's our luck – and I just have to say I do dislike the red tape, and I'm very much afraid it may be counterproductive.'

'Oh Angela, don't you threaten me too! Peter threatens to kidnap my dogs and now you say he'll steal more because we've tried to stop him stealing.'

'Come on, sweetie, no need to take everything so seriously. Peter was joking, and I only meant that he's a bit of a bolshie. What I was getting at was that maybe we should have another try at sorting ourselves out before more damage is done.'

'What kind of try?'

'Well – suppose you brought your Martin back at five o'clockish this afternoon?'

'He's not my Martin. What do you want Martin for?'

'I've a peace plan to put forward.'

'Are you playing games, Angela?'

'Games? I don't play games. And I don't fight, I don't pick fights.'

'Nor do I.'

'Oh well, forget it, love!'

'Have you really got something worthwhile for us to listen to?'

'I'm going to suggest that we leave you alone for ever.'

'Honestly Angela?'

'Come and hear me out this afternoon.'

'Very well. I'll ring you if Martin can't make it. I must fly.'

Olive flew back to the cottage and rang Martin. He sounded, first, relieved that her night had been undisturbed, secondly angered by the kidnap or rather dognap business, and thirdly sceptical of Angela's good faith. But he agreed that the chance of a termination of hostilities must not be missed.

'Interesting that she sees herself as non-belligerent,' he commented; 'it doesn't give confidence in her judgement or her idea of what's peaceful. But I look forward to our meeting, because I've got a trump card up my sleeve. Wait and see, if you can! Until five o'clock!'

They duly forgathered in the sitting-room of The Old Hundred at five, Angela, Olive and Martin, no Peter. Tea was ready, and Angela served it in the Crown Derby cups and offered round a plate of chocolate biscuits, which Olive and Martin refused.

Then Martin asked Angela's permission to switch on his tape recorder, and she replied 'Help yourself!' and began: 'I regret the trouble I've caused you, Olive, and you know how sorry I am about Peter's thick-headedness. After your dear father, my husband, died, you and I were saddled with his will – his fault, not ours. He had done his best for me – I wouldn't let him do more – but forgotten that Olive would be rich and I would be poor – and that's been the basic difficulty. I don't grudge Olive her money, after all I was responsible for making sure she got it and I didn't, but I couldn't quite bring myself to throw away my most valuable inheritance, the right to live at The Old Hundred.'

'Until you settled elsewhere – a temporary right,' Martin slipped in.

Angela smiled at him and continued: 'My James Crighton turned me into a wicked step-mother without meaning to, the dear old boy. The arrival on the scene of my teenage son made a bad situation worse – again, not my fault that he landed on Olive's doorstep.'

'But he's had his uses, materialistically speaking,' Martin murmured.

Again Angela merely smiled.

'To cut a long story short, a story that has two sides, Olive wants what's hers and doesn't want to share it with us. Sorry, sweetie, I'll rephrase that – there's pressure on us all to split up and buzz off. I've thought of a few alternatives, one or other of which might suit. Shall I go on?'

Martin nodded.

'I'd clear out immediately, taking Peter with me, and we'd both sign legal documents swearing never again to darken Olive's doorstep, if she'd pay me half the value of The Old Hundred and its contents – the contents as listed in yesterday's inventory.'

'A non-starter, Angela – Olive would have to sell The Old Hundred and her half of the contents in order to hand over such a sum to you – I happen to be in a position to know the cost

165

of your proposal. Have you another to put forward?'

'Yes. She could give me The Old Hundred – I would wait for it for the years that would free it from Gift Tax – or else she could leave it to me in a will she was unable to revoke.'

'Anything else? Is there anything else you're expecting to get out of your marriage to Sir James?'

'Why yes, Martin, there is something else. I'm prepared to go to law to have my husband's will rearranged as he originally wished it. Sorry, Olive, but I do feel it wouldn't be fair for me to be the loser when you're only the winner because of my say-so. I'm sick of being wicked – I won't be cast as the evil genius, having to listen to your scorn and insolence, Martin – and I think my stepdaughter should be ashamed of the way she's treated me, even after she'd been informed of my benevolence and in spite of all my friendly overtures. I'm convinced I'll get more in a law court than I will from you two.'

Martin produced a piece of paper from his briefcase and inquired: 'Shall I read it to you, Angela?'

'What is it?'

'I believe you're thick with a solicitor called Harris. He's an old rogue, but he's careful not to be caught breaking the law. You and he must have thought you could squeeze Olive by claiming her father had wanted to do more for you than he did, that you had kindly preserved her inheritance, and therefore she should reimburse you fully. It was or would have been a good confidence trick – you know how sensitive and generous Olive is. However, Mr Harris has decided not to commit perjury. Here is his letter setting out exactly what he did for Sir James, and the consequence is that the whole case you could take to law would be your word against his and against the mountain of evidence of Sir James' high principles and family feeling.'

Angela, no longer smiling, red in the face, appealed to Olive: 'Does all this claptrap mean you're rejecting my proposals and want to go on quarrelling?'

Martin answered her question: 'No, Angela – we're here to put a stop to the quarrel you've picked with your stepdaughter. You talk of taking her to court, but she's done nothing wrong, whereas you've admitted you were the accomplice of your son, who stole a desk from Olive, and you haven't denied that you were trying to defraud Olive of her inheritance. As for Peter, my duty is to protect my client from his unwelcome attentions either by agreement or by law. I think you should be looking for a different sort of deal, Angela, not for a favour from us, but to do us and Olive in particular the favour that might persuade us not to call in the police.'

'Olive,' Angela replied in a wheedling tone of voice, 'sorry, love, but I did warn you – and I can't afford to kiss you goodbye and leave it at that. I'll have to talk to the press, local and national if I can, and tell them the whole story, everything – everything, you understand?'

*　*　*

It was the morning of the next day. A kind of cooling-off period had been agreed by Martin, Angela and Olive; but no time scale was specified, Olive was far from cool, she was extremely agitated, and additionally vexed by disagreeing with Martin.

Her position, stripped of hesitancy and diffidence, was that she inclined towards capitulation. She longed to be free of the entanglement, whatever the cost – wealth meant nothing to her, she was not even devoted to bricks and mortar, and she could not bear a row, let alone a row without end. She was aware that she had been tricked and made a fool of by Angela, but was not willing to be hard on the woman her father had loved and married; moreover she herself had an obstinate affection for her stepmother. When she was a child she had always been ready to relinquish her toys to any other child who wanted them, and she now felt likewise. She was grateful beyond words to Martin, but she could not be so strong against Angela as he was, she would do anything in the world in order not to be pilloried in the press, and, to sum up, she was inclined to say: 'Take what isn't yours, leave me alone and to hell with you!'

Martin opposed her thus, but in the gentlest terms: Angela's blackmail was bluff – if she could interest the media in her story, which was unlikely, she could well be at risk from the laws of libel. Her alternatives were out of the ques-

168

tion – justice and injustice apart, they would draw Olive into legal minefields. Olive would have to sell The Old Hundred and share the proceeds if she wanted to help Angela, but whether or not the proportion of that share could ever be agreed was an exceedingly moot point. He objected to criminals getting away with murder, and wanted to remind Olive that she was capable of ambivalence in the matter – she was a pacifist at one moment and an avenging angel the next, and he was sure either that something completely intolerable would happen in the near future, or that she would act with incredible altruism and live to regret it.

Early that next morning Olive asked Peggy to keep an eye on her dogs while she returned her tray and perhaps had a word or two with Angela.

She began, almost standing in the kitchen doorway, by asking: 'Where's Peter?'

'In bed, I expect,' Angela replied. 'I don't know, I haven't seen him yet.'

Olive then embarrassed herself by eating humble pie in respect of yesterday.

'I'm sorry it got so nasty.'

'So am I, love – but lawyers always muddy the water.'

'Martin's more than a lawyer to me. I don't want you to be poor, Angela.'

'Thanks for the thought.'

'No, really.'

'I believe you, sweetie. But there's a big gap between your thought and my situation.'

Olive was struck dumb. She suddenly felt that

reconciliation was an illusion. Helplessness and hopelessness took over, and she replaced the tray and turned to leave.

A female shout followed by a scream broke the awkward silence. It was Peggy – Olive recognised her voice and ran out into the yard.

Peggy was galumphing towards the corner of the house, and she shouted at Olive: 'He's got Buddy!'

Olive understood and ran flat out in pursuit of Peter, who was making for his motorbike, holding the violently struggling dog with his two hands. The engine of the motorbike was turning over, ready for a quick getaway, and a black plastic bag lay on the ground beside it.

'Stop, Peter, stop!' she yelled at him.

By the bike he did so, he had to, he could not control Buddy, and after cursing he yelled back at her: 'You come closer, Olly, and I'll thro'le your puppy-dog, I'll thro'le the life out of him, see!'

She neither paused nor faltered, she ran straight up to him, took a wide swing with her right hand, and the heel of it connected with his nose – the sound of his nose breaking was audible. He dropped the dog, wailed with pain, shed blood, covered his face with his hands and called for Angie, who had observed the scene. Olive carried Buddy towards Shepherd's Cottage, while her face was being licked gratefully.

Angela said, 'Sorry, love,' as they passed each other – she was responding to Peter's cry for assistance.

Olive repeated twice: 'That's it, Angela.'

She and Peggy went into the cottage. Peggy told her story, then Olive rang Martin.

'You were right, I was wrong,' she said, and explained why she was doing as he had predicted.

The upshot was that an hour later Martin arrived at The Old Hundred, followed by a police car containing the two officers who had been there before. They entered the house, and half an hour later Martin was giving Olive an account of the steps he had taken.

'I've applied for a legal injunction, which means that Peter would be breaking the law if he trespassed on your property or troubled you elsewhere. Peter has been informed of my application in front of witnesses and on tape, so he can already be arrested for lifting a finger against you or doing damage of any sort. I've also informed Peter and his mother that we will be pressing charges against them both for theft.'

'Oh dear!'

'You can mend fences at a later stage. Money will heal a lot of their wounds, I fancy. But I cannot stand by a moment longer and let you be oppressed and ruined by that pair. I can't stand it personally, and I shouldn't stand it professionally.'

'How did they react?'

'Not well. Don't worry! Are you thinking of going to work?'

'Yes.'

'Well, I'll see you off. And this evening you

must come to my home, eat there and sleep there. That's as near an order as possible, Olive.'

'What will happen tomorrow? I can't continue to own The Old Hundred and be banned from going near it – I'll almost be another Peter.'

'Do as I say – we'll cross other bridges in due course. Please, darling!'

She was obedient. She put Peggy in the picture and locked the cottage. She got through the day and drove into Warminster, was greeted by Martin's mother and cried on her shoulder.

'Martin's been wonderful,' she said, 'but the fact is that they've won – or if they haven't won, nor have we. The Old Hundred's finished – I'll never enjoy it again, I'll never feel easy, I'll be apprehensive and guilty, probably both at the same time. It was such a happy home when my mother was alive! The locusts have gobbled up all the joy and the happy memories. I'm such a lucky girl – please forgive me for crying and complaining!'

The three of them dined together. Martin's mother made it a pleasant occasion. After dinner Olive expressed a wish to have a look at The Old Hundred, just a look from the bottom of the drive, by which she secretly meant a last look. Martin indulged her, and they drove to Luffield in his Rover.

The house was lit up. A party was evidently in progress, there were vehicles on the gravel sweep, lights glared from every window, light shafted out through the open front door, and loud rock music crashed into the balmy rustic atmosphere. The time was eleven o'clock, and figures seemed to be leaving the house and congregating round motorbikes and old bangers.

Martin had parked on the verge opposite one of the two paddocks.

'A final celebration,' he remarked.

'The dregs of Daddy's cellar, I expect,' Olive murmured back.

'I wonder what they're celebrating, his broken nose, or the end of their occupation of the house.'

'Won't they notice us watching them?' she asked.

'We have more right to watch than they have to notice us and object,' he replied.

A vehicle with a wonky exhaust pipe drummed down the drive and into the darkness with the aid of a single headlamp. Other cars and motorbikes followed. Soon the gravel sweep was empty and, although the lights remained on, peace descended on the scene.

'Have you seen enough?' Martin inquired.

'Yes,' she replied with feeling.

The explosion occurred as she spoke. The house blew up with a thunderous bang. The roof flew upwards, windows shot outwards, great tongues of blue and red flames obliterated the building, and a roaring wind swept in from nowhere – it was all over in seconds, but the fire burned on.

The watchers stood in the road. To be closer would have been impossible because of the radiating heat, and the same applied to rendering help. Martin was going to dial 999, but village people, joining them in the roadway, had already done so.

They stayed until the Fire Brigade had done their best, and had told them the explosion was probably caused by petrol in the cellar. They did not express a view as to how it could have happened. There were no survivors.

EPILOGUE

Olive was shattered by the sight she was seeing, and Martin too in his masculine way. They assumed that Angela and Peter were within The Old Hundred and were being burned alive. They were in no doubt that the fire was arson, that Peter had decided to make sure nobody would have the house if he and his mother were not to have it, and therefore they were witnessing a combined suicide and murder.

They stood where they were for about two hours. Martin offered to take Olive home, but she felt she had to be in at the death of her old home. Besides, the police wanted to take statements from herself and Martin, and they themselves had questions to ask after the first shock had slightly worn off.

What did the firemen mean by petrol, arson by petrol – how much petrol would be needed to cause such a huge explosion, where had it come from, where in the house would it have been stored, how had it been ignited?

The firemen had time to try to answer their questions – for an hour after the fire began they were unable to get near the house or the hydrants for fire fighting. They suspected the cellar had been awash with petrol, probably imported in tins over a longish period. Laymen, as a rule, have no idea of the explosive force of petrol, they explained, especially if the petrol was in a confined space; which is why people were so often burned by throwing it on a bonfire, they underestimated the range of the consequent flames, and again why cars and aeroplanes were apt to blow up. As for ignition, they guessed that somebody had thrown a match on the petrol – fuses with delayed action timers were a professional item, and the consensus was that they were looking at an amateur job.

What made the firemen think the arsonist was an amateur?

Well, their understanding was that a mother and her son in his teens were living in the house, and they had deduced that the fire was part of a domestic scrap.

Had they any evidence that the mother and son had been inside and were dead? Another possibility could surely be that they had left the house before the petrol exploded?

The firemen shook their heads. Judging by accounts of the party in progress, the departing guests, and then the bang, the residents would have had to run pretty damn quick in order to escape the fireball. The likelihood was that determination of whether anyone died in the fire, and who they were, would be up to the dentists.

Olive's tears flowed and dried on her cheeks repeatedly, and alternately she suffered from the heat of the fire and from an internal chill and violent shivering. For much of the first and worst phase she buried her head in Martin's shirt, but then she began to look sideways at the devastation and utter little whimpers as flames engulfed one after another of the parts of the house fraught with the dearest associations. The roof had gone but the joists, which were like the exposed ribs of a member of her family, burnt slowly and collapsed inwards in turn. She could see through an empty window space the wall of her father's dressing-room with its group photographs of his school-fellows, his comrades in the army, his political colleagues, and, when the fire subsided, stars in the night sky. On the ground floor the fiery tongues licked feverishly at furniture and furnishings – the sitting-room curtains burned well, and in her father's study the desk ran out of luck. She and her mother had listened to and loved their operatic favourites in the sitting-room. Her father had retired to his study during their binges of opera. Certainly art and love had been the preoccupations of her youth, although she was only a fancier and a fan of art, and her feelings for love were mere dreams. The Malones, the barbarians, had ousted beauty and filled her house with ugliness, and now the good and the bad of her history were reduced to a hot dust that stuck in her throat and itched in her eyes.

At some point she was agitated for a more positive reason. She had noticed that some branches of the sycamore and the oak tree in their respective paddocks were smouldering, and was afraid the fire could spread to the former farm buildings and catch Shepherd's Cottage. Martin urged her not to worry too much – the hoses were already spouting great arcs of water in the relevant direction. But her tapes, her recordings, were in the cottage, she retorted. They were replaceable, he would replace them, if need be, he said. But they were the recordings she had played with her mother, she told him – and then, realising she had erred on the sentimental side, she added: 'It doesn't matter, everything's done for, who cares!'

At another moment she became panicky in respect of her dogs. She had left them with Mrs East, and feared they could disgrace themselves if they were not let out into the garden. But Martin rang his mother on his mobile, and reported that the dogs were fine, asleep in their baskets, had been out and eaten a biscuit apiece.

At last she was ready to be driven away. The Old Hundred was no longer a house, it was four incomplete walls, it was embers turning into dust and ashes. She looked back at it with blurred vision, and apologised for sobbing again on the road to Warminster.

Her parting with Martin was not satisfactory – she could only thank him and hug him, she was not in the mood for kisses.

Olive stayed at Meridian Road for four weeks. Almost every day she said to Gwyneth East,

Martin's mother whom she now called by her Christian name, that she was overstaying her welcome; but Gwyneth would have none of it. She claimed that she was the grateful one, she and Winnie were grateful for the companionship of Olive and the partial loan of Olive's delightful dogs. The routine of the visit was that Olive was at work in the daytime, and spent evenings and dined with Gwyneth, or with Gwyneth and Martin quite often, and perhaps once a week with Martin at a restaurant. The atmosphere in the house was cosy; a daily lady, Rose, cleaned, washed, cooked lunch and prepared the evening meal; and everyone sympathised discreetly with her plight.

The fly in the ointment was Olive's attitude to her stepmother and her stepmother's son, who would be called her step-brother by pedants, both presumed dead.

She argued intermittently that she had murdered them, and implied or even hinted in her worst attacks of conscience that Martin had pushed them into a corner, from which their preferred means of escape was into the next world. She said it or as good as said it, and within a minute or two withdrew and denied it. She had not known she could be so changeable, apt though she was to be indecisive.

She should not have mistrusted Angela from the word go, and should have been more tolerant of that retarded and uneducated youth. Angela had all to gain and nothing to lose, Peter had his first chance in life, no wonder that they had plotted to relieve her of the excess of her fortune. Angela was a frightful liar, Peter would have raped his stepsister if they had continued to live at close quarters, but perhaps Olive would have preferred to put up with it all than to see them roasted for their sins.

She reasoned with herself, and both Easts, Gwyneth as well as Martin, reasoned with her. How could anybody guess that a dispute over property would end so badly? It would be too difficult to deal with daily life if you had to expect everyone you disagreed with to burn himself or herself to death before your eyes. Martin was convinced, and temporarily convinced Olive, that Peter Malone was not committing suicide, far from it, his intention was to wreck The Old Hundred, to harm and hurt its owner, and he died of his own stupidity and incidentally killed his mother.

A different approach to the Malones was unimaginable, Martin said, except by reference to the repudiation of worldly goods, the laws of the land, human nature and the instinct of survival. He had not been convinced that Olive was fully prepared to disinherit herself by giving Angela her home and the wherewithal to live in it: was she ready for penury? He had brought in the police and requested the law to protect her because he was not sure how far beyond his established criminality Peter would go – neither as her solicitor nor her lover could he expose her to the risk of confinement and violent death. Peter's past threatened Olive's future, she must see that, and Angela had used Peter as her instrument to achieve her objective, she obviously summoned Peter to reduce Olive to pulp, and they nearly succeeded.

But Olive's toes still stuck in memories of her peculiar friendship with her stepmother. Angela's method of conning her was somehow to reassure with those smiles, those encouraging endearments, and her self-control and cleverness. She could see why her father loved Angela, yet was ashamed not to have laughed at the accusation that they had once played the lesbian game together. She had been unconscious, it was silly – and she was silly to have feared her exposure in the gutter press: why would anyone be interested?

In retrospect she worried that she had exaggerated everything, and drawn Martin into a conspiracy that could look suspiciously like filial jealousy, or the grabbing of the lion's share of family spoils, or neurosis or spite or homicidal mania. No, he said – no, he repeated, and patiently rebutted over and over again her opinions, and revealed the misconception of her regrets.

At the end of the four weeks the Coroner's Inquest was held in Warminster. It established that Angela and Peter, and only the two Malones, had died by misadventure, but that others had played a part in the conflagration and would be dealt with elsewhere in due course. Peter Malone had apparently invited his cronies to a party with a difference at The Old Hundred, not a bottle party, but a petrol party, and in return for bringing along a gallon or two of petrol they were given things in the house, bits of silver or china, small pictures. These cronies were aware that a fire would be started, both Peter and Angela spoke openly of it, but no one expected it to get so out of hand or to be so awful.

After the Inquest, Olive expressed a wish to return to Shepherd's Cottage. She felt in need of time and solitude to reorder her thoughts and recover her equilibrium. Gwyneth urged her to postpone the move, but, in character, having not been sure what to do or when to do it, Olive was adamant once her mind was made up.

Martin had learned from experience. Now, instead of begging her not to move out, instead of arguing or raising any obstacle, he cooperated with her in word and deed. He drove her back to The Old Hundred, was careful not to comment on her brimming eyes or white face, and helped to tidy up the cottage and prepare it for her to sleep in as soon as she felt inclined. They visited Peggy, who was pleased to know Olive was returning to Luffield.

She drove herself over in the evening of the next day. When she said goodbye to Martin in Meridian Road, she thanked him with warmth and they kissed.

He rang her in the evenings, the four following evenings, at the cottage. During the fourth call she rather wished he would leave her alone – they had seen so much of each other lately. But on the fifth evening he did not ring, on the sixth she missed him, and on the seventh she rang Gwyneth East and asked if Martin could be given her love. He rang her again.

He also invited her out to lunch. He said he could and would like to give her lunch on any day. She excused herself, she had such a lot of work at the Surgery to catch up on, she postponed acceptance of his invitation. He said he understood. But then, in the course of an evening chat on the telephone, he mentioned the better weather that was forecast and she remarked that it would be nice at Stonefield. As a result they had lunch in the garden of the pub at Stonefield with the tinkling stream and willow trees.

He never crossed her, or pushed her in a direction she shied away from, or failed to encourage her to do as she pleased. She did not want to meet men from insurance companies who wished to assess in financial terms the damage done to The Old Hundred. She wanted to play no part in the prosecution of the lads who had assisted Peter to burn down the place and received property stolen from her for doing so. Martin undertook to deal with these matters on her behalf. He supported her without question or obvious reservations.

One day he referred to the restaurant where they had danced and she changed the subject: he was careful not to ask her out to dinner.

The basis of the inhibition that introduced novel difficulties into their relations was that she thought she could not marry Martin. Fear of giving herself to a man not only physically, but with the emotional totality of the monogamist that she knew she was, restrained her – Martin might turn out to be like her father, remote as the possibility appeared to be at present. She loved Martin, potentially if not yet practically. She loved him more than ever – did he, would he, reciprocate her consuming kind of love? Further scruples revolved round the Malones, their fate, and how it came about.

Martin had been the driving force that precipitated the fire. She shuddered to recall his firm blocking of all of Angela's and Peter's exits. He was tougher than she had expected. What if he were to be tough and even vindictive towards his wife?

Yet she was neither forgetful nor unjust. She remembered, and owned up to herself, that he had only acted in her interests, with her approval in principle, and to save her body and even her soul from the destructive influence of her stepmother. She recalled the alarmed and alarming manner in which her heart had sunk as Angela had seemed to engulf and be actually drowning her, and the terrors of her life in the proximity of Peter.

That Olive could not shift the whole burden of blame on to Martin's shoulders somehow irritated. Her conscience pricked the more because she felt unfair to innocence as well as having been murderous to guilt. Yes, the Malones were guilty, but, she half-thought, Martin was not so innocent as she had hoped he was – he was not much better than herself.

The end of her inner arguing was the frustrating admission that she was too confused to reach a conclusion in respect of Martin, and she lived in minor dread of being subjected to any form of cross-questioning.

One especially sweet summer afternoon at Stonefield, in the sunshine in the almost deserted garden, he proposed to her.

It was tactful beyond her imaginary requirements, its tactfulness disarmed her. He simply said: 'I'd love to marry you when you've got nothing better to do. No answer, please – please say nothing – no pressure – forget it!'

As a result she immediately explained that she was honoured and flattered, but could not say yes, was sorry but she could not, although she was fonder of him than of anybody else in the whole world, he was her best friend, and she could not bear the thought that her refusal would make the slightest difference to their friendship.

He understood. She was a trifle suspicious of his ability to understand her – was she being manipulated? She preferred understanding to misunderstanding; but the next thing she did wrong, which she was afraid he would find as incomprehensible as she herself did, was to kiss him long and tenderly on the lips before she hurried to the Fiesta and shot off towards the Surgery.

That evening he rang and spoke to her in his customary strong and sympathetic way. He discussed his housing arrangements with her. His mother was growing old and would need full-time care at some stage. His flat in the family home would come in useful for a nurse-companion, and he ought to think of removing either to another Warminster house or to a house in a village like Stonefield. To live within walking distance of his office would be nice, on the other hand to live in a village with a post office, a shop and a pub might be nicer. What did she recommend? She answered cautiously, although she had a vested interest in the subject.

In the succeeding days he carried on exactly as before. He telephoned, he met her for lunch, he was neither embarrassed nor embarrassing. She relaxed little by little, although her inward arguing took a new turn and stress that was not bargained for accumulated.

She was free. She could see that in a final and harsh analysis she had been freed of her two tormentors by death, and that if they had survived they might never have let her go. She could envisage horrors beyond those conjured up by Martin, for instance that Angela would have presided over the games Peter was set on playing with her. Moreover she was free of the later threat of matrimony. She could almost trust Martin to take no for her final answer.

The trouble was that he was going to need a woman – not herself – to look after the house he was about to buy.

* * *

She grew jumpy with him all over again. She hoped he would not revert to his proposal, yet worried that he did not do so. She was sad not to be able to face Gwyneth East, who would probably urge her to think again. She was upset by Peggy, who would keep on telling her she could not live alone in Shepherd's Cottage for the rest of her days.

Desperation lurked round every corner of her imagination. The decision she eventually arrived at was that she owed Martin a much fuller explanation of why she had rejected him. It was brave by her standards, and shaky in accordance with her temperament. But at a certain lunch in Stonefield she broke a silence to say a bit breathlessly: 'That restaurant you took me to, is it still open?'

He replied without emotion that it was, and asked if she would like to try it again.

They agreed a date, and she was convinced she had taken a step far too close to the edge of the precipice.

She somehow survived the intervening days. But for Martin's sake she was determined to be clearer and kinder than she had been the first time round.

Dinner was a strain for her, although he appeared not to notice anything amiss. When the music started, she suggested a dance in a tremulous voice. He was amenable, hardly enthusiastic, and on the dance floor he held her at a respectable distance. She had planned an embrace during which she could justify herself by whispering logical sentences into his ear. But she felt she had to do it somehow if it was the last thing she did, and she started to stammer unfinished phrases.

'Martin ... You know ... I can't, I couldn't ... I must say ... Oh don't look at me! ... I'm sorry, Martin ... I can't!'

'Are you trying to tell me you can't marry me?' he asked mildly.

'I was ... but ...'

'You don't need to say a word more. Nothing's changed for me either. You're still the girl I love and would love to marry. You're the best girl in the world, that's my opinion. But I'm never going to bother you or make a nuisance of myself.'

'Oh thank you! I just want you to know ... How can I say it? ... I haven't been myself for months, not since my mother ... and Angela and Peter in the fire ... so many mistakes...'

She cried. He drew her closer to comfort her. He did not say anything, he did not need to. By means of some supernatural or hypernatural power he seemed to heal her – it was as if he woke her from a troubled sleep, as if he raised her up from a nearly moribund state. Peace broke out within her, conflict belonged to bygone times, the book of the past was closed, mourning was done. Her spirit was refreshed and even renewed, and she stopped crying, drew away from him, looked straight at him and said in a voice tinged with wonder: 'Oh Martin!'

'Olive?' he queried, sounding startled. 'Is something wrong?'

'No. I know at last what I want to say. Do you remember my telling you I loved you more than anyone? It was true, and it is. I haven't changed either, for a change I'm not being changeable – but everything's different, I've made up my mind, and I could promise I won't change it again.'

'Olive, I don't understand.'

'Well, perhaps you've been too understanding.'

'What am I supposed to say?'

'I leave it to you, Martin, I leave all to you.'

'Will you marry me?'

'I don't deserve to be asked – I don't deserve you – but I don't mean no – please, if you can, if you will, please, please!'

They thanked each other. They kissed each other. They danced and drank champagne, and strolled in the moonlight and spent a long sweet time in the Rover, and drove back to Warminster as dawn glimmered over in the direction of The Old Hundred.

Olive told Martin a story during that drive. It was the story of Donna Anna and Don Ottavio in Mozart's opera *Don Giovanni*. Donna Anna, she related, loves Don Ottavio, who is a wonderful man, has loved her faithfully and has been her support after she was assaulted and her father was murdered. Yet at the end of the opera she responds to his proposal of marriage by asking him to wait for her for another year.

'I never liked Donna Anna for that reason,' Olive said. 'I don't think she should keep Don

191

Ottavio waiting. Martin, forgive me – I should-
n't have behaved like Donna Anna, I shouldn't
even for a few days, but at least I've seen the
error of my ways, and intend to do my best, to
seize the chance you've given me to spend my
whole life doing my best, to make you happy
ever after.'

RINGLAND 13/10/03

ROGERSTONE 23/4/04.

MALPAS 23/10/04

RINGLAND 10/5/05